by
Nicole McInnes

Holiday House / New York

ACKNOWLEDGMENTS

Sending a book out into the world is, in so many ways, a team effort. These are the people I want to thank for being part of the journey:

Superhero literary agent Stacey Glick, whose enthusiastic professionalism set this novel on its path toward publication.

Editor extraordinaire Sylvie Frank and the folks at Holiday House. From my first correspondence with Sylvie, it was clear that Brianna had found the perfect home.

Writing cheerleaders Dani McInnes, Joan McInnes, and Cathy Price for always being supportive.

Beta readers Nancy McInnes, Corwin Leonard, and Haley Leonard for always being perceptive.

Teachers over the years whose love for the written word greatly influenced my dream of becoming a writer. The list includes, but is not limited to, the following: Albert "Cap" Lavin, Martha Allen, and Sheila Girton (Sir Francis Drake High School); Ron Hansen and Page Stegner (UC Santa Cruz); Ann Cummins and Barbara Anderson (Northern Arizona University).

My very first teachers, Nancy McInnes, Don McInnes Jr., and Don McInnes the Taller, without whom I would not have been exposed to half of the amazingness I've been fortunate enough to experience in my life.

My children, Jonah and Sarah, who regularly take that amazingness and multiply it by a hundred simply by being who they are every day.

Printed and Bound in December 2012 at Maple Vail, York, PA, USA.
The text typeface is Berkeley Oldstyle Book.
www.holidayhouse.com
First Edition
1 3 5 7 9 10 8 6 4 2

Library of Congress Cataloging-in-Publication Data

McInnes, Nicole.
Brianna on the brink / by Nicole McInnes. — 1st ed.
p. cm.
Summary: A one-night stand has life-altering consequences for popular, sixteen-year-old Brianna, who must then accept help from the one person closest to her mistake.
ISBN 978-0-8234-2741-3 (hardcover)
[1. Pregnancy—Fiction. 2. Home—Fiction. 3. High schools—Fiction. 4. Schools—Fiction. 5. Popularity—Fiction. 6. Grief—Fiction. 7. Family problems—Fiction.] I. Title.
PZ7.M478654Bri 2013
[Fic]—dc23
2012015961

For my family.

Contents

1

what not to do

HERE'S A LIST of what not to do when you're sixteen (and a half) and the guy you just went all the way with keels over from a heart attack on the floor of your sister's house:

1. Don't run screaming down the street in your underwear.
   Don't—I repeat: Do *not*—do this, no matter how tempting it might be. Things will only get much worse much faster if you do, and also you could end up being responsible for somebody dying unsupervised.
2. Don't call his wife immediately.
   Duh. Besides, the moment Derek's heart stops I'm still under the impression that he's single. Kind of like how, the moment *before* his heart stopped, he thought I was twenty-one. Let's just say it's complicated and leave it at that.
3. Don't assume he's only kidding and head into the kitchen for a bowl of Cherry Garcia, thinking he'll apologize later for freaking you out.

Of course you want to believe it's just a big prank when somebody falls over like they've had a heart attack. And of course you want his face to stop changing all those patriotic colors (from red to white to blue), because that is just flat-out creepy before it turns flat-out terrifying. And it's only natural for you to want him to turn to you and say "Gotcha!" or "Kidding!" or something like that.

Anyway. The room I rent at my sister Keisha's house is tiny. It was meant to be a laundry room, but Keisha and her boyfriend, Robby, keep the washer and dryer in the carport so they can rent the space to me. Well, "rent" is kind of a strong word for it, I guess. Basically, I wash the dishes, water the plants, and occasionally cook mac and cheese or noodles in Styrofoam cups for the three of us, and they let me stay. It sounds really nice of them, but honestly, the room is about the size of a tampon box.

I know something is wrong for real the second Derek sits up and shakes his head. "What the hell am I doing?" he says, more to himself than to me, and before I can answer—or even decide if I *should* answer—he scoots away toward the edge of the bed. Then he stands up for exactly one-point-five seconds before crashing to the floor without making a sound (other than a big *thwhack* as his head hits the bedside table). And believe me, nothing will make you feel helpless and alone faster than hearing someone's head do that.

I jump out of bed with the sheet clutched to my chest and crouch down next to where Derek is wedged between the bed and the wall to see if he can tell me what's wrong. But then I realize he can't do that because he isn't breathing, much less talking. So I shove the bed as far away from him as I can (a few inches max) and do my best to remember the CPR steps we learned in health last year. But I can't really remember them, and it isn't long before the whole thing starts to feel like a bad dream where everything moves in slow motion.

When I can tell for sure that Derek's lungs aren't going to start back up on their own, I run into my sister's kitchen and dial 911, because one of the things that sucks the most about having no money is not having a cell phone when I really need one. Normally I'd call Keisha herself (even though I know for a fact she'd beat the crap out of me for hooking up with a guy in her house), because she's cool as ice in a crisis. She and Robby are camping in Sedona for the weekend, though, which means there's no way for me to get ahold of her. And, sadly, there's no point whatsoever in calling our mother, Jolene, who lives only ten minutes away but who's about as useful as windshield wipers on a submarine because she's basically a walking crisis herself.

I hold the sheet closer to my chest and try to convince my fingers to stop shaking long enough to press those three magic numbers on the old wall phone with a twisty cord long enough to stretch into every room of the house. That cord is what lets me keep an eye on the doorway of my bedroom, and I watch Derek for any sign of movement while I wait for someone to answer. The sheet is still warm from what the two of us were doing in bed just a couple of minutes ago—not just hands and mouths at that point, but shoulders and bellies and thighs. Then I hear the 911 operator saying, "What's your emergency?"

After that, there's not much. I don't remember crying to the 911 operator that we needed help or telling her where I lived, but I must have done both because within a couple of minutes someone is pounding on the front door, and then the paramedics are right there in the house with me. They push in through the entryway and run through the living room with these big suitcases that I can only assume have all sorts of tools inside for bringing the newly dead back to life. I read their name badges as they shove past—Alec, Tony, Michael—and I know Keisha will gladly murder me if they break anything like the little ceramic penguin figurine Robby gave her on their second date. The penguin has a crazy grin on its face, and it's holding a big heart between its flippers. It's supposed to be a heartwarming declaration of love, but it's always skeeved me out.

And here's something you really don't want to have happen when you're sixteen (and a half) and the guy you just went all the way with keels over from a heart attack: you don't want the paramedics to start yelling at each other because Tony's "not moving fast enough" and Alec "needs to get his shit together and have the resuscitation kit totally prepared" after they clean out the rig. You don't want to have to scream, "In there! He's in there! God, please don't let him die!" while you point with a hand you can no longer feel to the room where a man is dying or maybe dead already.

You definitely don't want to have all the paramedics turn and stare at you like you're some little know-nothing skank wrapped up in a ratty bedsheet, the back of your hair all tangled so they know exactly what landed that poor guy on the floor of the bedroom in the first place.

And, you know, I can totally see how stupid of me this is, but even at that moment, with all those paramedics running around and the red cherry light from the ambulance flashing through the front window of Keisha's house, part of me is thinking things still might work out okay. I'm thinking the paramedics will go into the bedroom, do their thing, and then laugh in relief when Derek sits up and says, "Where am I? What's going on?"

And I'll be able to laugh right along with them while I shake my finger at Derek like a full-grown woman—like somebody's mother—and say, "You really gave us a scare, mister."

But that's not how things go at all, because I'm nowhere close to being a full-grown woman.

2

next of kin

THE PARAMEDICS are yelling—at me, at Derek, and at each other.

"What's his last name?" one of them—Tony, I think it is—asks me as the other two kneel over Derek and take turns pumping at his chest. "Come on! Come *on*!" they're shouting. They've already had to drag him out into the narrow hallway to do CPR, since they couldn't all fit in the laundry room.

"I don't . . . I don't know," I answer. "I barely know him." I can hear how high-pitched my voice is, but there's nothing I can do to bring it down to normal.

"Do you know his home phone? Anyone we might call? Next of kin—you know, a close relative." Tony says this like I wouldn't know what "next of kin" means.

"No," I say. "No." The truth is I only met Derek a few hours ago, though one of the first things I said to him earlier tonight was that he looked familiar.

Maybe we're kindred spirits, he said, looking right into my eyes. *Maybe we met in a past life.*

Tony starts going through the pockets of the pants Derek was wearing before he wasn't wearing them anymore. They're khakis, and I allow myself a couple of seconds to remember how I unbuttoned them after we got to Keisha's house, letting them fall to the floor while we stood next to the bed, our mouths already finding each other, me already trusting him completely.

"Got some ID," Tony says, holding a brown leather wallet up to the other two, who are sitting back on their heels and breathing hard (*Why are you stopping?* I want to scream at them).

Michael nods, wipes his forehead. "We got a pulse," he says, "but it's thready. Let's load this guy the hell up."

At some point after that I must have thrown on my clothes and grabbed my purse, because the next thing I know I'm trying to get my sister's old beater of a Nissan started. The paramedics have already closed the back doors of the ambulance, and I frantically turn the key in the ignition while pounding the steering wheel with my other hand and saying the magic words that I'm pretty sure got Derek's thready pulse back—"Comeoncomeoncomeon . . ."

At the same moment the Nissan groans to life, the ambulance pulls away from the curb in front of me, siren blaring. It takes me forever to get the car up to fifty, but that's how fast I'm going (in a twenty-five-mile-per-hour zone) when I finally catch up to Alec, Tony, and Michael and blast through the last red light before the hospital right behind them. When they turn into the Emergency Personnel Only lane, I drive around the crowded patients and visitors lot, the half-bald tires squealing, until I finally find a space. After that, it takes only seconds for me to sprint across the pavement toward the ER entrance, where glass doors whoosh open to let me through.

There's a check-in station just inside the building, and I keep running until my hands hit the narrow counter and my breath fogs up the security glass. An overweight woman with bags under her eyes sits typing at a computer on the other side of the window, and I tap on the glass to get her attention. She looks at me for a second, just long enough to open the window a few inches, and then her eyes go back to the screen. "Can I help you?"

"Is he okay?" I demand. "Is he alive?"

"Patient name?" she asks without even bothering to look away from the monitor.

"Derek," I say, panting. "Derek . . . I don't know his last name. But they just brought him in. Tony and Alec and . . . I don't remember the third guy's name."

She looks at me then, looks at me with pity or impatience, I can't quite tell which. She probably deals with people like me every day. "You're obviously not family."

I look down. "No." And as soon as I say it, I know I should have lied and said yes. But maybe lying would have added more bad luck to this night, which already seems to be overflowing with it.

"You can sit over there," tired typing lady says, jerking her head toward some plastic-covered chairs and benches. "Nurse'll come out and tell you when there's news."

Most of the people in the waiting room are staring up at a TV mounted high on a wall like they're ER regulars, like this is just something they do on Friday nights. And I can see why, because the place is somehow comforting, with its fluorescent lights and neutral wallpaper, even if everyone here is either scared or sad or angry or in shock. It's almost like the building was made big enough and strong enough to hold the worst feelings in the world. Some people stare into the air in front of them with no expression at all, snapping out of it only when the Authorized Personnel Only doors next to the check-in desk swing open and a nurse comes into the waiting room to call out a last name. I find a seat near the glass doors and sit there watching Conan with the others.

Every once in a while there's a *whoosh* to my left as someone new comes in. Sometimes they come in all relaxed—happy, even—as is the case with a homeless-looking guy with a bandage on his hand who calls out, "Hey there, Maggie," to the woman at the check-in station before taking a seat. And sometimes there's a huge, noisy rush, like when a bald guy comes in screaming that the stab wound he got last week is infected and will somebody please put him out of his misery *now*. He's holding his side, his tear-streaked face scrunched up in pain, and our eyes meet for half a second as he looks around for someplace to sit.

And it is during that half second that my own tears finally come—tears of fear and stress and exhaustion and not knowing what to do next other than just sit and wait while Conan's audience laughs in the background. A Navajo lady sitting on the bench to my right and decked out in generations, probably, of family turquoise passes me a box of tissues without saying a word.

After about twenty minutes, a doctor and a nurse come out through the Authorized Personnel Only doors, their heads tilted toward each other. Both have paper masks hanging under their chins, like just moments before they pulled them from over their mouths but haven't bothered to take them off. The doctor says something in a low voice to the nurse, who nods and looks around the waiting room. Maybe they're looking for someone who belongs to Derek, I think—someone, anyone, other than the teenage girl sitting next to the exit, the girl with smeared makeup, messy bed hair, and G-U-I-L-T scrawled across her forehead in invisible ink.

"Plain," the nurse calls out, but nobody in the waiting room stands.

Instead, as if in response, the glass entrance doors of the ER open again.

I glance up and see, of all people, my English teacher. And my first bizarre thought is this: *The school must have heard I was in trouble, and the counselors must have been busy, so instead they sent Plain Jane* (not her real name, obviously).

She is moving fast, unwinding one of her endless scarves from around her neck and looking around like she's lost something, her eyes wide. "Did you say Playne?" she asks the nurse, who nods. "Well, I'm here," Plain Jane says. "Where is he? Where's my husband?"

My second thought is *Oh, crap. Now I know where I've seen Derek before.*

Plain Jane still hasn't seen me sitting there, but I know she will if I don't do something quick. So I stand up, looking at the floor so my hair falls over my puffy face. I can hear the doctor and the nurse speaking to Plain Jane in low voices as I move toward the exit.

And I'd be home free at this point if it wasn't for Maggie, the check-in lady, who slides open her glass security window and points at me. "She's here for him, too," Maggie calls out to the three of them, no doubt thinking she's doing me a favor.

The next thing I hear is "Miss?" It's the doctor, calling to me.

But rather than answer him, I keep walking, ignoring all the eyes and thinking some new magic words: *You don't see me, you don't see me, you don't see me*. Slipping through the doors, I leave a trail of soggy Kleenex behind me as I hit the parking lot and break into a run.

3

wildflowers

MONDAY MORNING the news is all over Percival Lowell High:

Did you hear about Mrs. Playne's husband?

He was only twenty-five.

Do you think it was a suicide? (I don't know, but can you imagine being married to her?)

Do you think she killed him?

During homeroom Mr. Gupta announces that an informal memorial service will be held at lunchtime, and counselors will be available for students who might be traumatized by the news. My friend Jules Hill, who sits in front of me, turns around and rolls her eyes. "Yeah, like I'm so upset I don't think I can handle school today," she whispers. "In fact, I better take a mental health week."

"Ha," I whisper back, trying to sound convincing. Because Jules doesn't know anything about what happened Friday night after I left the club with Derek. Nobody at school does. Not yet, anyway.

I hang out with Jules because she's kind of a bad-girl cheerleader like me—and because I wouldn't be nearly as high up on the food chain if she hadn't plucked me from certain social doom in the girls' bathroom the first day of freshman year. Still, Jules can be a little scary sometimes. The way she likes to take charge of situations and people, it's almost like she got too much testosterone in the womb or something. We like to joke that someone in the school office must not have gotten the memo that it was a really bad idea to let us share even part of our schedules, since both of us are constant distractions to everyone—especially the guys and especially on spirit days, when we're required to wear our red-and-white Lowell High cheerleading uniforms. Mine has the initials BT on the chest, and Jules has JH on hers. We always like to add a little something extra, too, like black fishnet stockings and stick-on Power Ranger tattoos on our thighs, because we both know that making an impression is key. It lets everybody—the cheer squad, the football team, and the rest of the student body, even those who say they couldn't care less about cheer—know who we are. One day at practice I overheard the football coach and his assistant laughing about us being "vixens." And when they saw me watching them, they looked away, grins sliding off their faces.

"Seriously, though," Jules says after first period, "poor Plain Jane." She almost sounds like she means it, which I know can't be the case because Jules prides herself on being compassion-challenged. It's midmorning break, and we're perched on our hallway railing—the one right across from our lockers that should really have our names engraved in the steel, since everyone else knows not to even think about sitting here.

Jules pulls out a compact and checks for hairs above her upper lip, stretching her mouth from side to side in the tiny mirror. "So, what did you do this weekend?" she asks me.

I shrug, try to look casual. "Nothing much."

"Well, I haven't talked to you since you left the Frog with that *guy* Friday night," she says, and I detect something behind her wicked smile. It's the same annoyance, the same rivalry I sensed on Friday. She hides it quickly, though, and snaps the compact closed. "You better give me all the gory details, by the way."

"Ha," I say again, needing to dodge the interrogation that's sure to follow. I've already spent the entire morning trying to ignore the sick feeling rolling around in the pit of my stomach since late that night, about an hour after I got home from the ER. That was when the police knocked on the door of my sister's house. I think their exact words were "We just need to ask you a few questions about the deceased."

"Derek's dead?" I must have been in shock, because even though I could hear myself saying those words, I couldn't quite figure out what they meant.

They asked me how old I was, and I said, "Almost seventeen." I knew telling them I was older, like I'd told Derek, would be pushing it. The female officer—her name tag said AHRENS—asked if there were any adults present in the house.

"My sister is usually here," I told her, "and her boyfriend. But they're out of town." The other officer—QUINN—pulled a notebook and pen from his shirt pocket, and then both of them sat with me at the kitchen table as I cried into my hands and told them an abridged version of the story: "I was out with some friends and this guy offered to give me a ride home. I invited him in, and the next thing I knew he was having some sort of attack. That's when I called 911."

"And the sheet?" Officer Quinn asked. He'd stopped writing in his notebook and was frowning at me.

I pretended to draw a blank. "The sheet?"

Officer Ahrens stepped in. "According to the paramedics' report, you were wrapped in a sheet when they arrived on the scene," she said.

"I . . . I was changing." God, I was a lame liar.

"Was Mr. Playne changing, too? Was that why he wasn't wearing any pants?" asked Officer Quinn.

"Tom," Officer Ahrens said, placing a hand on his arm and then looking me right in the eye until I caved.

"We fooled around a little," I admitted. "I thought he was a college guy."

They both stared at me then until I said, "Please, I haven't done anything wrong. He acted like he didn't feel quite right, and then he just stood up and collapsed on the floor, which is when I called 911."

"We're not saying you did anything wrong, Brianna," Officer Ahrens said. "But it's our job to ask these questions."

"I know," I mumbled, staring down at my hands. "I understand."

"Do you mind if we take a quick look around?"

I told her I didn't mind and then showed them the laundry room, so they could see where it had all happened. Maybe I needed to prove to them that I hadn't set out to kill anybody, that I hadn't set out to do anything other than connect with somebody.

After going in there, the officers didn't have anything more to say. I was afraid to ask if I was a suspect, because that might be a suspect-sounding thing to say, so I said nothing. Officer Ahrens gave me her card and told me to call if I had any concerns. She said they'd file a report and that would probably be the end of it unless any other questions came up.

The end of it, I thought. *Not for me, it won't be.* Because I was already thinking of the hell I would go through at school when the girls I'd been with Friday night figured out Derek was the guy flirting with all of us at the Frog. From there it would be no time at all before everyone at Percival Lowell High figured out who Derek was and how he'd died. I had already considered not going back to school ever again, but that would basically have been a total admission of guilt.

Before walking out the door behind her partner, Officer Ahrens suggested that I see someone. "Like a therapist," she said. "This type of thing can be very traumatic, especially for someone your age."

"Okay."

"You take care of yourself, Brianna," she said. "You hear?"

I didn't bother to tell her that I had spent pretty much my entire life doing just that. Instead, I simply nodded and closed the door behind them.

At lunchtime, Jules wants to check out the memorial service, so we head over to the flagpole, where a podium has been set up and the principal's getting ready to say a few words.

Someone has enlarged a picture of Derek and Plain Jane to poster size and attached it to an easel from the art room; Derek's smiling eyes watch from that poster as Jules and I approach. Scattered on the grass all around the easel are little bunches of wildflowers students have picked from the patch next to the football field. I'm grateful Plain Jane is nowhere to be seen, and I overhear a student asking one of the counselors where she is.

"Administrative leave," the counselor says. "Otherwise known as grief leave. The last thing anyone needs to deal with after a major loss is a bunch of rowdy teenagers."

While Jules and I stand there, some of the teachers get up to say a few words about Derek, like how they met him once at a school function, or how he and Mrs. Playne were such a lovely young couple. The biology teacher mentions that we should all keep Mrs. Playne in our thoughts during this difficult time and that those of us in her classes need to be extra calm and supportive when she comes back in a few weeks. I wonder what calm and supportive would look like coming from me. Maybe I can offer to sharpen pencils or clean the whiteboard after class. Maybe I can leave a note on her desk on my way out of the room: "Sorry about having a one-night stand with your husband that ended up killing him."

"Hey," Jules says, stopping in front of Derek's picture. "He looks like the guy . . ." Her voice trails off, and then her head whips around so she's looking right me. "Oh my God, Bree. That *is* the guy."

"Shhhh," I say, knowing that the thing I've dreaded has arrived and that my secret will be officially out of my control in the next, oh, five minutes or so—however long it takes for Jules to get to our next class after lunch, which is English. It's Plain Jane's class, and both Charlotte Kimura and Kimmy Valentine take it, too—Charlotte and Kimmy, best friends and Jules's original groupies, who are not only on the squad but who were with us at the club when Derek first appeared.

"That's the guy who was hitting on you Friday night," Jules is saying, her voice full of shock and awe.

"Shhhh!" I hiss again, loudly enough this time for the principal to stop midsentence and frown at us.

"Oh my God," Jules says again, pulling me away from the crowd and back toward our railing. "You *left* with him. Wait a minute." Her expression is pure, evil glee. "Did you—did you *do* him to death?" She'd probably say something worse if half the teachers in the school weren't staring after us by this point.

"Seriously, Jules," I mutter through clenched teeth, picking up the pace to get us away from the gawkers as quickly as possible. "Shut *up*." And I know right then I'm pushing it, because you really don't talk to Jules that way.

She doesn't get mad, though. Instead, she just grins at me as we head toward our lockers, clearly knowing a good story is on its way. And I can practically see the wheels turning and the gears shifting in her head as we stop at our lockers. "Spill it. *Now.*"

"I will," I tell her, looking around nervously to see if anyone has overheard. Getting the police off my back was nothing compared to what it's going to take to fly under these teachers' radar. Most of them have it in for me, anyway. "Just don't assume anything. Okay?"

"Yeah, right," she says as we grab our books and head toward English. But I can tell she's drooling to know more. That, for once, I have power over her instead of the other way around. I don't have much time to enjoy the feeling, though, before—

"Hey, Jules. Hey, Brianna." It's Nathan Lumpke, who I've known since seventh grade, standing front and center, right in our path. Nathan Lumpke, über-geek and total fashion-backward hot mess combo standing there all big-eyed and shaky at being in the Presence. Nathan practically founded the unofficial Brain Tribe at Lowell, and he wears button-down shirts daily, like every good brain does. He puts his own special twist on the look, though, by going around with the top four buttons undone to show off his chest (which is as pale and hairless now as it was in junior high). He's also fond of slicking his hair straight back like a greaser from the 1950s, affording me and Jules a great view of his forehead pimples, several of which look like they've gotten some good squeezing recently.

"How are you lovely ladies doing today?" Nathan asks us, and if I wasn't so distracted I'd have to give him credit for at least trying to be something he's not, which is a smooth-talking player.

"We're hotness itself," Jules says without missing a beat. "Obviously."

"I can see that," Nathan says, nodding as he looks from me to Jules and back again.

"Yeah, you keep dreaming, Lumpke," Jules says, laughing, as we walk past. "Keep exfoliating, too." I know it was my job to add that last part, but I'm not up to it. Not today.

We've already been told there will be a sub for English, which is a good thing—I don't think I'd be able to keep it together in front of Plain Jane, who is the last person on earth I want to face at this moment, other than my sister, Keisha.

And, walking into the classroom, I'm right back at the first day of the school year when Jules and I walked down the hall, reading off our schedules to each other. "Comp 2," I said. "Room 301. Teacher: Playne, Jane."

"You've got to be kidding me," Jules said.

"It's on your paper, too," I told her. "Look right there."

"Playne, Jane," Jules repeated, staring at her schedule. "Can you imagine the hell she must have gone through as a kid?"

"But what do we know?" I said. "She's probably some gorgeous sex goddess."

"Yeah, our competition, right?"

Jules was *so* not right. Jane Playne lived up to her name 100 percent. Even though she was in her midtwenties and had only been teaching high school for a few years (which meant she should have been fresh and on top of things), she was almost as much of a disaster as Nathan Lumpke: long, straight hair hanging in her eyes with no styling whatsoever, no makeup (not even a swipe of lipstick, for God's sake), and don't even get me started on the clothes. We're talking shapeless brown dresses and these awful clogs that made her look like one of the peasant women digging for potatoes in the Van Gogh painting we were forced to study in art. I could tell right away she had decent bone structure and some real potential under all the blah, but she did absolutely nothing to use it. That first day, walking past her desk toward my seat, I noticed a framed picture of Playne-comma-Jane and some hot guy who for some reason had his arm around her, which didn't seem right.

Plus, she knitted. Like a fiend. Which was also just . . . wrong somehow. Halfway through that first class she gave us a writing assignment: free-write for fifteen minutes about your summer vacation. Yeah, right. I kept thinking I heard a clicking sound, and when I looked up from the note I was writing to Jules, our new teacher was knitting a scarf out of thick yarn. This would have been weird even in the middle of winter, but in August? After telling us our free-write time was up, Plain Jane looked around the room and then down at her roster.

"Brianna Taylor?"

I looked up from my note again—I was drawing a cartoon hairball with hands holding a pair of knitting needles—and I stared at her like, *Excuse me?*

"Do you want to read an excerpt aloud from your free-write, Brianna?"

I just ignored the question completely, rolling my eyes and then staring right at her again like, *Back off, loser,* until she looked away and moved on to someone else.

As soon as that first English class was over and we were back out in the hallway, Jules turned to me and said, "Guess we know who this year's victim is, right?" Because there always had to be a victim—one teacher we tortured above all the others, one teacher whose life we turned into a living hell without actually getting in serious trouble for doing so. As Jules said, what better way to break up the mind-numbing monotony that was a normal day at Lowell High? First came the planning stage and then, usually sometime after winter break, the execution of said plans. Last year, after enough old-school tricks like thumbtacks on the seat and KICK ME signs taped to the back of his jacket, it was pretty clear we were the ones responsible for the resignation of Mr. Ribaldi, our geometry teacher. I felt kind of bad about it, but since he never said anything (probably because he was too embarrassed to admit to being bullied by a couple of cheerleaders), we never got into trouble.

"I don't know," I told Jules now. "Plain Jane's almost too much of an easy target."

"There's no such thing," she said, frowning at me. "What are you, a *nice* girl all of a sudden?"

"Please," I said, trying to sound as self-assured as Jules. "You wish."

"I don't wish anything," she fired back. "You decide to start acting all goody-goody, and I'll just make *you* the victim." She smiled, but it was a wolfish smile, canine teeth showing and all. Jules could be like that; if she didn't have your back, you'd better *watch* your back.

Neither one of us could have known on the first day of junior year that I would turn out to be the master at making Plain Jane's life a living hell—that being a goody-goody was the last thing I'd have to worry about.

4

nothing like a kid

I WASN'T LOOKING for anything the night I met Derek. I went to the Laughing Frog because I was finally getting used to my brand-new life as a junior, and so I went for the same reason the other girls on the squad did—to blow off some steam and give thanks to the cheerleading gods that I'd lived through another night of flying through the air like some kind of human football.

I used Keisha's old fake ID to get in because she looks just like me in that picture. It wasn't hard to steal it, since Keisha keeps it in the top drawer of her dresser, but I still felt a little twinge of guilt as I plucked it from the drawer. I was careful not to disturb the other stuff in there—her lace thongs, her birth control pills, the switchblade she'd probably use on me if she found out I'd stolen the ID and very carefully changed the birth date to a more realistic year. So far, though, she hadn't noticed it was gone.

The football game had been intense that night, more intense than usual because it was the game that would decide whether or not our boys went to regionals. The field lights seemed brighter, the brass band horns seemed louder, and judging by how amped the entire squad was, you would have thought we were carrying bullhorns as we yelled out our cheers. Right before Braden Lewis scored the final touchdown, the crowd was on its feet, because at that moment everybody knew we were going to win; they could feel it in the electrically charged air. I could feel it, too, up at the top of the pyramid. The lights were hot on my face, and Charlotte's and Kimmy's arms trembled a little as they held my feet. *Don't blow it, girls,* I thought, still smiling, just before they launched me into space, where I became a red-and-white missile—everybody's dream girl performing her flashiest pike basket toss. Jules was my main spotter. She high-fived me when I landed, then said, "Damn, girl," which meant a lot coming from her, since she doesn't usually give out compliments.

So, the good news was we won that night (handed Truman High's asses to them on a platter was more like it). The bad news was that our entire football team went home right after the game to rest up for regionals, which meant they wouldn't be at the Frog to keep all the college guys from trying to sit at our table and buy us drinks.

"Boo-hoo," Jules said as we flashed our fake IDs at the bouncer and walked straight up to the bar. "No one to protect us." We'd all changed out of our uniforms, but I knew the electricity of the game was still clinging to us, making us look somehow more sophisticated and confident than we really were. Jules caught the eye of the bartender and said, "Sex on the Beach, please." Then she turned to me. "Just, you know, 'cause you gotta love a drink with a name like that."

"I do?" I said, but I was laughing. That's how it always was: Jules came up with the one-liners, and I got the honor of being her sidekick, the front-and-center recipient of her wit and charisma.

"Yeah," Jules said, jabbing me in the side with her elbow. "Maybe we'll find you another Ian tonight."

I laughed again, but it was forced this time, because the

reference to Ian Colson stung; Jules had picked him out for me sophomore year, since he seemed nice and a little naïve (which meant he was a perfect victim for me to practice my vixen moves on). And he *was* a nice guy—a nice guy who genuinely seemed to like me. I was all about impressing Jules, though, by pushing things with Ian too far, too fast, and after I used Ian up and tossed him aside like a tissue (Jules thought it was brilliant), he transferred over to Truman High.

Behind me, Kimmy—squeak-toy blonde to Charlotte's cool Japanese American mystique—looked around like a kid in a candy store. "It's raining men," she said, and as soon as we found a table and sat down I thought, *Here we go,* as some college guy appeared and started talking to Charlotte. Turned out his coat was just draped over the back of her chair, though, and he'd come over to get it.

"Sorry for the interruption," he told us as he retrieved the coat and turned back to the bar.

"It's no interruption," Jules called out to him. "What's your name?"

The guy stopped in his tracks and turned around. "What's yours?"

"Oh, I like him," Jules whispered, nudging me with her elbow. Then she lifted her chin, flashed the guy her sexiest halftime-routine smile, and said, "It's Jules."

When he smiled full-on right back at her, I noticed he was actually older than college-age. There was a quiet coolness in his expression that made him look more comfortable in his skin than most college guys I'd met, and it also made me instantly paranoid that he was really an undercover cop. I started to rummage in my wallet for Keisha's ID as proof that it was okay for me to drink the two-dollar Jell-O shots Kimmy had ordered for us. Jules sensed my anxiety and said, "Cool it," out the side of her mouth. She was right, of course. Making such a rookie move would have made me look even more underage than I was.

"We're resting up before midterms," Charlotte told the guy, pathological liar that she was capable of being. "You know, at the university."

"I assumed," he said, looking around at all of us. When those calm eyes got to me, they stopped. "So what are you girls majoring in?"

"Anthropology," Charlotte said. She had dated college guys before and knew about stuff like that. "We're juniors," she continued (which was technically true). I had a hard time believing he'd fall for it.

Next to me, Jules took a big gulp of Sex on the Beach and then fixed her eyes on the guy. "Care to buy some hard-studying girls a few drinks?" she asked him.

"I don't know," he answered. "It looks like you're pretty well set."

Kimmy got all flushed, which always happened when she was nervous. She started giggling, too, and saying stuff like "How much money do you think he *has,* Jules?," which made the guy smile.

I had to admit he was handsome, in a classic, J.Crew kind of way. Also, he was remarkably unskeezy for a guy halfway flirting with four girls in a bar. His hair was cut, his hands were clean, no meth teeth, and it almost seemed like he didn't care whether we liked him or not. I guess it all came down to that cool-eyed confidence, which might have been what made me feel pulled toward him the way I did, no matter how hard I tried not to look interested. It wasn't long before my unintentional stare-fest was broken by Kimmy's pep rally voice saying, "Brianna! Dude, take a picture. It'll last longer."

The guy must have noticed my staring, too, because within

seconds he was crouched next to my chair, holding out his hand like we were at some kind of meet-and-greet. "I'm Derek," he said, little tan crinkles forming at the corners of his blue, blue eyes.

Watch it, Bree, I told myself. It occurred to me that he hadn't yet introduced himself to anyone else, but I took his hand anyway and shook it. Of course, I rolled my eyes at the same time, just to show everyone how clearly bogus this all was. But God, here's where I admit it. He was more than just kind of handsome: he was gorgeous. "You look familiar," I told him, trying to maintain my cool.

"Maybe we're kindred spirits," he said. "Maybe we met in a past life."

"Whatever. I'm Brianna."

"But everyone calls her Bree," Kimmy giggled, and I wanted to say, *Enough already. You sound like a complete moron.*

Derek was looking right into my eyes again—or trying to, anyway—but I kept looking away, kept looking down at the empty shot glasses and thinking about the little zit in the crease of my nostril. I tried ignoring him, but I kept not being able to stop myself from smiling. It was ridiculous.

We sat and talked for a while and I told him all about myself (none of it true, of course—I told him I was twenty-one, that Charlotte had gotten it wrong because I was majoring in psych, not anthropology, and that I rented a house with some other students. That last part was only a partial lie). The other girls watched, and I thought they looked a little awestruck. Well, everyone except Jules looked awestruck; Jules looked mostly annoyed.

Then, out of the blue, she changed the look to Totally Fine with Everything and turned on the charm again. "So, Derek. Where's your favorite place to be kissed?"

"The nape of the neck," he answered without even pausing to think about it.

I could tell Jules was a little disappointed, that she'd been hoping he'd say something dirtier, but she got up from her chair anyway and came over to where Derek was crouching. "Alrighty then," she said.

"What are you—"

"Just drop your head down," Jules commanded, batting her eyelashes.

"Uh... okay." He glanced at me before letting his head fall, exposing the back of his neck as Jules bent over him, her blond hair draped all around his shoulders. *Is this girl for real?* his eyes asked.

I just rolled my eyes and shrugged in reply, tried to keep from smiling. Because with Jules, anything goes.

"Yeah, um... wow," Derek said when she'd finished kissing his neck and had pulled him back to standing.

She turned him around to face her and looked up at him. "Now do me," she demanded.

"Uh, I don't really think—"

"Oh, come *on*," Jules said, giving Derek's shoulder a little, flirty shove.

"What is this, Truth or Dare?" he laughed.

"Totally," Charlotte chimed in with the usual mischief in her voice. "Truth or Dare."

"I dare you," said Jules. She spun around and backed up to Derek, lifting a handful of her kinky blond hair and offering up her own nape.

Obediently, Derek bent his head forward and touched his lips there for half a second. "Happy now?" he said as Jules released her hair, letting it fall down her back.

And no matter how cool she was trying to be, I saw her eyes roll back in their sockets before she turned around to face Derek again. Kimmy and Charlotte saw it, too, and we all got really quiet, because it was like some line was being crossed here, almost like we shouldn't watch, but how can you take your eyes off something like that?

Not that I cared. It wasn't like I'd tattooed PROPERTY OF BRIANNA TAYLOR on Derek's forehead. I didn't even know this guy. Jules flirting with him was no problem whatsoever. Really.

"I *dare* you to try that on Bree," Kimmy shrieked, completely caught up in the moment. "She'll *die*."

And I should have just gotten up and gone to the ladies' room at that point, since I could pretty much tell what was coming by the amused look on Derek's face. I didn't leave, though. Instead, I sat there like I was glued to my chair, felt the heat coming off Derek's body as he stepped closer and announced in an exaggerated stage voice, "I am up for this challenge!" Then he bent down and whispered, "That is, if you are." Like we were in this together.

Charlotte and Kimmy cracked up, but Jules just went back to her chair and sat down, looking bored now, like we were all suddenly wasting her time.

I wanted to have the perfect comeback for Derek, wanted to say "No way" and "Yes, please" at the same time. Most of all, I felt my age, felt too young, at the exact moment that I wanted to feel just the opposite. At that moment, more than anything, I wished I had the kind of mother who had prepared me for this, who had told me what to do when a guy who obviously knows what he's doing is coming on so out of the blue that you might not be able to resist the riptide of him if it pulls any harder.

But I didn't have that kind of mother, and when Derek whispered, "So, what do you say?" it felt like the most natural thing in the world to simply lift my hair off my neck for him and drop my head forward like if I'd let strangers do this sort of thing to me a thousand times before.

s looked away, but Charlotte and Kimmy sat up a little straighter in their chairs. "Ooooo," they said in unison, and when I glanced out from under the drape of hair at Derek, his eyebrows were raised in surprise this time. Then he leaned closer, moved around behind me, and touched his lips lightly and softly right at the base of my neck.

"What is up with your friend Jules?" he whispered into my skin, chuckling a little. And the words felt like bunny fur. His stubble was the only hard thing about the sensation, and the touch of that scratchiness made all the little hairs on the back of my neck go *zing!*

Even though the kiss lasted only a second, an unnerving silence followed. All the girls—even Jules—were looking at me with their mouths hanging open, waiting for some juicy reaction, no doubt. And because I didn't want Derek to know he'd gotten to me, I decided to create a distraction. "What if I told you I was really just a kid?" I asked him, putting on my best poker face.

He stood up quickly and stepped back, looking freaked out. "*Are* you a kid?"

"Well," I said, glancing around the table at the girls. They weren't giving my secret away, and I was *this close* to having second thoughts about how I was going to answer. "No, but . . ."

"You act nothing like a kid," he said, finishing my sentence for me. Then he smiled and continued, "But I'll let you girls get back to socializing."

And then he did the thing that was probably the turning point for my heart and guts because I didn't expect it: he walked over to the bar, straddled a stool, and sat with his back to us. My insides did a sad little flip as I watched him go.

"That guy could be, like, a total pedophile," Kimmy whispered when he was gone.

"Whatever," said Charlotte, rolling her eyes. "He's hot."

Kimmy was looking at me a little nervously. "He was totally into you, Bree."

"Whatever," I said, echoing Charlotte and looking down at the table so my eyes wouldn't give my disappointment away.

"I swear I've seen him somewhere before," Charlotte mused to no one in particular. Then, apparently done with Derek's desertion of us, she changed the subject. "Man, I can't believe I have to drive my mom's minivan while the Honda's getting its brakes redone."

"At least you have a working car," I told her, happy for the change of subject. "Keisha's stupid Nissan's dying again, and this time I think it might be permanent."

"I can give you a lift." It was a male voice coming from behind my left shoulder, and I didn't have to look any farther than Kimmy's grin to know who it was, to know he'd come back. "Sorry," Derek said. "I left my drink here and just happened to overhear—"

"First your coat, and now your drink," Kimmy said, looking at him with deep suspicion. "How convenient."

Charlotte cut Kimmy off and glanced in my direction long enough for me to see that little sparkle in her eyes. "That would actually be great," she told Derek. "If you take Bree home, we'll have room to pick my brother up from work."

"What the—" I started to say, but Charlotte shushed me. Meanwhile, Kimmy looked utterly confused, because we all knew Charlotte didn't have a brother.

"You know, Bree," Charlotte continued, clearly enjoying the ruse. "My brother . . . uh, Norman."

"Oh, right!" Kimmy practically shrieked. "Norman!"

Even though Jules wasn't objecting to Charlotte's trying to set something up between me and Derek, I couldn't help wondering if she'd try to punish me for horning in on a situation that should have been hers. But I didn't horn in. *Maybe Jules will just get over it and be cool with the whole thing,* I thought as I glanced at her and then at Derek. *After all, it's not like she doesn't have a bazillion other guys falling at her feet.*

"It's no problem to give you a lift," Derek said. "Really." He knelt down beside my chair and was looking right into my eyes again, staring until I started to feel that familiar numbness in my head.

"Okay," I said, going along with the whole thing. "Say hi to Norman for me," I told Charlotte. It was all I could do to unhook my purse from the back of my chair and stand up, and I knew the Jell-O shots were only partly to blame.

"Don't do anything I wouldn't do," Jules said. She winked as I pushed my chair toward the table, and it seemed at that moment that she'd decided to be okay with this. Still, Jules's hands were wrapped a little too tightly around her empty glass, and there was something in her expression that I knew I'd have to pay for eventually.

5

that particular fantasy

THEY SAY the worst thing that can happen to a cheerleader is flying from the top of a pyramid and not getting caught on the way down. I became a flyer as soon as I hit the varsity squad, and I can't count the number of times this almost happened to me during practice. Either the spotters were zoned out when they should have been paying attention, or the choreography got messed up and someone wasn't where she was supposed to be. Also, if you're not keeping your whole body tight while focusing on your spot, you can end up in a wheelchair. All of us on the squad knew about that girl from New Mexico who was helicopter tossed at the regional semifinals, and for some reason nobody caught her on the way down. That cheerleader's neck was broken, and she'll never walk again. Ever.

Still, being a flyer is an honor, and I never should have gotten this far in cheer, not with my background. I remind myself of it at every practice and every game, too. Because girls like me, girls without the "right" parents and the "right" clothes and the "right" situation, almost always end up super-invisible or super-stoned or super-slashed up and down the arms or all of the above, depending on how good we are at making do with what we have.

It was Jules who helped turn things around for me back on the first day of freshman year. Sure, it didn't hurt that the legendary Keisha Taylor—feared and admired for her quick temper and her beauty—was my older sister, but Keisha had already graduated and wasn't there to ease my transition into the new world of high school.

So there I was, friendlessly clutching my hall pass in the girls' bathroom as I stared at myself in the chipped mirror and thought *Hello, ugly* for the hundredth time that day. I had just endured a hellish end to junior high that involved both heartbreak and the private, lonely ache of invisibility—never being noticed by the boys I liked and never feeling cool enough to make friends with the popular girls I admired from afar—and I had no idea how to change things now that I was a freshman. It was a toss-up between hiding in that bathroom a little longer and getting a spine already and stepping out into the main corridor.

Before I could choose, one of the stall doors flew open, and Jules Hill—the girl who would soon be voted Hottest Freshman Currently Breathing Oxygen by the football team—came out with a cigarette clenched between her lips. "Don't tell," she said, hiking up her leggings with both hands and then crushing out the cigarette on the bathroom sink.

She looked at me in the mirror while she washed her hands, and I could have just gone into an empty stall at that point. Instead, I stood there frozen while she dug around in her purse and then pulled out a pink bottle of Fantasy, which she spritzed all over herself. I breathed in deeply, as if perfection might be catching.

"Takes away the cigarette stink," Jules Hill said to the mirror. Then she glanced at me. "You know, you're awfully quiet, but you do have something," she said. "A look. I don't know what it is exactly, but you should get some decent clothes and learn how to do your makeup. Awesome hair, by the way. Dudes are gonna dig you." Then she did something kind of bizarre. She turned toward me and touched my head for just a split second before walking out of the bathroom, and I remember thinking it felt like a sprinkling of pixie dust by the Bad Girl Fairy.

Things started turning around for me not too long after that, no doubt because I did what Jules said: I learned how to do my makeup (not too heavy on the eye shadow, liner and black mascara on the upper eyelids only, lipstick just a shade darker than my actual lip color), and I got some decent clothes (from the thrift store, yes, but I'd spend hours in there, digging through the piles of outdated jeans and sweater vests like Keisha taught me until I found things that accentuated the positives and cost nearly nothing). At lunchtime and between classes, I'd see Jules Hill and her two perma-groupies, Charlotte and Kimmy, patrolling the halls. Even though Jules hadn't said two words to me since the first day of school, I'd force myself to be brave anyway by holding up my hand to the three of them in occasional silent hallway greetings. Sometimes they'd do the same.

Then, one day toward the end of freshman year, Jules walked up behind me as I tried to keep an avalanche of crap from falling out of my locker and said, "You trying out for cheer?"

I wouldn't have been more surprised if she'd asked if I was planning to travel to the Amazon and join a tribe of cannibalistic pygmies. "I really wasn't planning on it," I told her.

"C'mon," she said. "You're not bad-looking, and I'm sure you can move, right?"

"Yeah," I said. "I guess so." Keisha and I hadn't spent all those unchaperoned childhood years grooving to the Motown and pop stations on Jolene's little plug-in radio for nothing. Keisha was always the choreographer and the star of the routine, and I was always her backup dancer. "Sure, I'll do it," I told Jules, holding my locker closed so she wouldn't see the crap avalanche and decide she'd made a mistake by talking to me.

"No chickening out," she said.

All four of us—me, Jules, Kimmy, and Charlotte—made the squad, and I walked back and forth every day between the field and the apartment where I lived with Jolene. It was worth it, because I loved cheer more than I'd maybe loved anything, ever. I loved being part of a group, and I loved the energy, and I loved that all those moves I'd learned with Keisha as a kid could finally be put to good use. By the middle of summer we'd all learned about a dozen routines, and when cheer season officially started in the fall of sophomore year, Coach Kristy promoted me to flyer because I was small and light, which I knew probably had more to do with my growth being stunted by Jolene's partying while she was pregnant than anything else. It was something my mother liked to brag about whenever she saw one of those PSAs about not drinking or smoking when you're going to have a baby.

"Pssh," she'd say, swatting the air with her hand. "I did all that stuff when I was knocked up, and you girls turned out fine."

By then, Jules had decided she could be seen in public with me on a regular basis—that I could be a stand-in groupie whenever Kimmy and Charlotte weren't available. Shortly after that, Jules and I started hanging out on our rail together, and it wasn't long before she started referring to Kimmy and Charlotte as "my stand-ins, for when you're not around."

I was sure they'd both hate me for taking their spot in Jules's limelight, but they had each other and pretty much shrugged it off. One day I realized they were walking a few paces behind me and Jules at lunchtime and between classes, and they kept doing it, day in and day out, until it seemed like the way things had always been.

As I walked out of the Laughing Frog with Derek, I thought about how fast things could change and how good it had felt to know I was worthy of being Jules's number one friend. I felt something similar now that I was with this older guy, though I understood it was probably more than just Derek's calm confidence making me feel this way. There was a good chance it was also the whole father issue thing drawing me to him in the first place. Because even if he wasn't nearly old enough to be my father, he did seem like the type who would be protective and encouraging and all those things good dads are supposed to be.

Maybe if I was on the Dr. Phil show, Dr. Phil would pass me a box of Kleenex and ever so gently tell me that Derek was really a replacement for the father I never had and for the mother I do technically have but who has never been there for me the way a mother is supposed to be.

Then there would be a tearful reunion after the father I'd never known walked out from behind a curtain and onto the stage.

Here's the only problem with that particular fantasy: my real father doesn't even know I exist, because Jolene (she never liked being called Mom or Mommy, even when Keisha and I were little) left him about three-point-five minutes after the pregnancy test came back positive. To hear her tell it, my real father (the sperm donor, she calls him) lived in his head the whole, short time they were together, always lost in his own world of dreams and schemes—"Things you can't touch," she called them. "Things that aren't worth anything. Plus, he wasn't exactly motivated to get a job," she'd say. "And I wasn't about to be saddled with a deadbeat *and* another kid. Hell, I wasn't much more than a kid myself when I got knocked up."

Jolene has always been honest that way. Kind of like how she was honest enough to tell me (on the morning of my sixteenth birthday) that I was cramping her style and it was time for me to move out of her house. That's how I ended up living in Keisha and Robby's laundry room. Was it a coincidence that Jolene's boyfriend had asked her to marry him the day before she said this to me? I think not. If there was any doubt before then that her boyfriend, Larry, and I were competing for Jolene's attention, it disappeared when he did that.

"Did you hear the good news?" Larry asked me in the kitchen that morning as I waited for my toaster waffle to pop up.

"News?" I said, but he just smiled.

That was when Jolene skipped into the kitchen and flashed her ring at me. "Sucka!" she hollered. And I mean, seriously, what mom says stuff like that?

"Oh, happy birthday, by the way," Larry said, smirking (I'm sure of it) as he snaked an arm around Jolene's waist.

I don't know what made Jolene prouder—the fact that Larry had given her a ring or the fact that they had been dating for a whole two months, which was without question some kind of record for her. But it's not like proposals were anything new for my mother. I've actually lost count of how many fiancés she's had over the years. None of them had ever given her a rock like Larry had, though. Most of the rings up to this point had come from the clearance cases at Target or Walmart, and they were never worth much when it was time to resell them at the Jumbo Pawn. Jolene made sure I knew Larry's ring was nothing like the others, that it was something special. Apparently, the proof of this was the fact that the ring was big and shiny and that it came in a velvet box with the word GENUINE printed on the top in gold ink.

"Well, uh... congratulations," I told the two of them as my waffle popped up. I had spent the entire morning getting ready for my appointment at the Motor Vehicle Division, and I wanted to get there early for my ten o'clock driver's license test slot.

But then Jolene shooed Larry out of the kitchen and said she needed to talk to me about something. "I've found the man of my dreams, Brianna, and I'm not about to screw this up by having a teenager around." With that, she grabbed some papers from the counter and handed them to me. "No offense or anything."

"None taken," I said. "What's this?"

"That," she said, grinning, "is your ticket to independence."

I looked down at the first sheet of paper, which had "So You Want to Become an Emancipated Minor" printed across the top. Below that were the words "Emancipation Workbook and Petition."

"You'll be on your own, girl. What do you think? Exciting, huh?" When she could tell I was having trouble picking my jaw up off the floor to say anything, Jolene just let herself ramble on. "Look. I've done the mom thing, Brianna. Now it's time for me to focus on me. I just kind of... want my life back, you know?"

I didn't even bother answering. What was there to say? And if she'd "done the mom thing," I had definitely missed it. So I just stood there with the toaster waffle in one hand and the emancipated minor papers in the other, wondering for the millionth time what kind of mother would say something like that to her daughter. The fear of being forced into legal adulthood at sixteen and not having a clue how to go about it must have been rattling around somewhere in my brain, but at that moment all I could think about was why I couldn't have the mother of my dreams, or at least a mother who pretended to care.

"Fine," I finally managed to say. "But can you at least come with me to the MVD so I can get my license?"

Jolene did come with me (sighing the whole time that she had "so much to do to get ready for the wedding"), and I did get my license, and the next day I had to move out because Larry wanted to use my bedroom as an office for his home-based business.

"What kind of business?" I asked.

"Don't be so nosy, Brianna. It's a World Wide Web thing."

"It's called the Internet."

"Don't be snotty, either."

"Fine," I said. I was using that word a lot lately.

Later that afternoon, as I hauled my sorry ass and my sorry backpack full of clothes and makeup through my sister's front door, Keisha said, "Well, at least she's straight with you. And she's getting what she deserves with that Larry idiot. No job, drinks all day. What a loser."

I didn't dare point out that Keisha's boyfriend, Robby, pretty much did the same thing—he just substituted pot for alcohol. Robby was one of those people who stayed at a job only until it started "killing his soul."

"Happy birthday, by the way," Keisha said as I dropped my stuff in the middle of her living room.

Everything about Keisha and Robby's little rental is old because that's the only kind of place they can afford, what with Keisha being the main breadwinner and working at the Stop'n'Shop. She's also been a stripper, a bartender, a vet tech, and just about every other job you can imagine, which means she has all sorts of random knowledge that actually comes in pretty handy sometimes. She can be like a guard dog when she wants to be, but there's also the other side of her personality, the one-strike-you're-out side, where she can turn on you, neck fur up and teeth bared.

I also knew that my big sister placed a high price on loyalty above all else—though I had to admit it sometimes seemed like she placed that price mainly on other people's loyalty to her, and not the other way around. That was probably why she and Jolene barely spoke to each other except when they absolutely had to: Keisha had given up on our mother a long time ago.

Part of this had to do with the time when I was eight and woke up in the middle of the night to find one of Jolene's boyfriends (boy-*fiends,* Keisha called them back then) taking pictures of me while I slept. When I told Keisha about it the next morning at breakfast she got a look in her eyes that could have cut through stone. And when Jolene let the loser move in a few weeks later, Keisha said, "Child Protective Services is going to take me and Brianna away from you if they ever find out what a total perv this guy is."

Looking back, I can see now that Keisha was giving our mother a warning: *Either you watch out for Brianna, or I will, even if it means getting the law involved.*

The next thing I knew, the perv was gone, his stuff piled on the front step when he came back to the house later that day. There was a note taped to the top of the pile saying the sheriff would be called if he so much as thought about trying to get back in the house. The note was written in Keisha's thirteen-year-old cursive, and when Jolene found out, she was *pissed:* "You have no right!" she yelled at Keisha. "You have no goddamn right!"

Sure enough, the guy was back the next day, standing in the kitchen when I got home from school. "Hello, Brianna-Banana," he said, staring at me with the corners of his lips curled up in a way that made my skin crawl. Earlier that morning Jolene had promised me we'd go to the park after school, but she was asleep on the couch in front of her soaps.

"Let's not wake her up," he said, holding a finger to his lips. "I'll take you to the park." I guess I could have said no, and I knew Keisha would be seeing bloodred polka dots when she found out he was back in the house, but the truth was I'd been waiting to go to the park for days. I was also afraid of the gangs who sometimes hung out there, and I wasn't about to go alone. So I went with him, and he watched me climb around on the monkey bars and slide down the twisty slide. At one point I let him push me on the swing, and I laughed as I soared through the air, telling him to push me higher. But then he started laughing right along with me and pushing the swing a little *too* high, until my own laugh turned into more of an out-of-control, scared sound than an I'm-having-so-much-fun sound. He pushed me higher and then higher still toward a turquoise Arizona sky, and when the unthinkable happened and I finally went up and over the crossbar of the swing set, the sound coming out of my mouth wasn't anything close to a laugh anymore; it was a scream. Then I couldn't even make that sound because, for an endless moment, I was upside down, suspended from that too-blue sky with my pigtails pointing toward the ground. The metal links dug into the flesh of my palms as the swing and I made a complete revolution over the top of the swing set before shimmying down through the air face-first. Once I was close enough to the ground that it wasn't going to make a huge difference *what* I did, I simply let myself fall. I landed in a heap in the tanbark below, one hand still wrapped around the chain in a death grip. When I looked up through my tears at Jolene's boyfriend, he was frozen in place like an ice statue, and the first words out of his mouth were "You told me to push you higher!" Like he was the kid and not me. Like the whole thing was somehow my fault.

Back at the apartment, Keisha asked me in an undead kind of voice where I got the blisters on my hands and the scrapes on my knees, and I told her. The next day I came home from school to find a lady sitting in the living room with Jolene, who was pressing on her eyes with a wad of tissues.

"What's going on?" I said.

The lady introduced herself as Susan and told me she was a

social worker. She said Jolene needed to work on some things but that Keisha and I would be okay, that people at the county agency where Susan worked would make sure we were looked after while Jolene did what she had to do to become the best parent possible.

Jolene said, "You have no right to take my babies away," which was weird, because she had never talked about us that way before. Then she reached for me, held her arms out while still sitting on the couch like it was all too much for her, like she didn't have the strength to stand up. "Bree-Bree," she wailed, and I almost looked behind me to see who she was talking to, because in all the years I'd been alive I had never once heard her call me that.

And Susan said, "Brianna is going to be fine, Ms. Taylor."

The perv disappeared during that month when Jolene was getting her head straightened out and Keisha and I were in the custody of Child Protective Services. Like all the kids in the temporary CPS dorm where we lived during those weeks, we had to go to Group. Group was held in the dim basement of the dorm, and it was where we were supposed to share our feelings. I remember the facilitators always passed out bagels and juice boxes, and all us kids would sit munching the bagels in silence. I don't think I said a single thing during Group the whole time we were living in the dorm, and Keisha told me she didn't say anything in her Teen Group, either. We'd see each other a few times a day during meals. Neither of us made friends. And then one day Susan showed up and told us we could go back home. And now, when I think back to that month, most of it is just like gray smoke in my head, like maybe it didn't really happen at all.

Keisha was the one who started teaching me how to keep life from eating me alive once we were out of the dorm and back with Jolene. Keisha was big into tough love, and she was big into making me tough, too, so I wouldn't be "steamrollered by life," as she put it. Still, I get why Keisha and I are a little messed up. And I thank God or Allah or Buddha or whoever's in charge up there in the sky that I never became a Worst-Case Scenario—so screwed up by a lousy parent that I can barely get through the day. I see those kinds of kids at school—pillheads popping whatever they can find in their parents' medicine cabinets, Goths wearing black clothes and white makeup 24/7, and huffers who have too few brain cells left to be bothered with something as basic as personal hygiene. I'm not one of those kids. I mean, I am and I'm not. I've got the weird living situation, the lack of real parents, and no clue what I'm supposed to do with my life. But here's what Keisha taught me about growing up the way we have: you can let it wreck you, or you can make it work for you. You just have to take control to survive. Jules knows this, too, and just like my sister, she refuses to be pushed around by anybody. Yeah, maybe I was quiet and shy for years after that, and maybe I didn't fully come out of that shell until I met Jules freshman year, but I made it through being a little kid.

6

playing field

"CAN WE JUST drive around?" I asked Derek once we'd left the Frog. The inside of his car smelled clean and comforting, like man soap and old leather.

"Sure," he said. "Anywhere you want to go is fine with me."

I didn't have anything particular in mind, but I did know why I wanted to drive. It was because ever since I could remember, riding around in a car and looking up as trees and telephone cables floated past the window had soothed me when I felt anxious or restless. And there had been something restless growing inside me that night, something prickly bouncing around between my hips and my heart ever since I'd (a) watched Derek kiss the back of Jules's neck, and (b) felt him kiss the back of mine.

Maybe the restlessness also had to do with the fake identity I'd created for myself as Derek and I sat at the table and talked. That was when I'd decided I liked not being who I really was for once.

Eventually, we ended up at a late-night coffeehouse downtown; we found a table for two in a dim corner where we could just hang out without either of us feeling like we had to say too much. Sounds completely boring, I know, but the truth is, there was nothing boring about it. Time moved fast that night, and I felt like I didn't have to worry about what was coming next. At one point, I grabbed a pen from my purse and drew a little sketch of Derek on my napkin, because I've always been pretty decent at art. When I showed him the finished product he nearly choked on his coffee.

"I wish I was handsome like that," he said.

"You are."

Which, I'm not totally sure, but I think it might have made him blush a little bit. Then he asked me to give him the pen so he could draw me. He got all serious about it, shielding the napkin with one hand so I couldn't see and sticking the tip of his tongue out the side of his mouth in concentration. It took forever, and I just sat there still feeling this *thing* crackling—only now it was crackling between two of us. *Wow,* I thought after he'd been drawing for five minutes. *He must be really good.* Then he moved his hand away and turned the napkin around so I could see the masterpiece he'd created. It was the simplest of smiley faces—round circle head, dot eyes, dot nose, and curved-line smile—and I laughed so hard in the middle of a gulp that latte foam shot out my nostrils.

Then, out of the blue, Derek said, "I wish I could go back and relive my college days. I was far too serious."

"Get outta here," I teased him.

"No, it's true. I was always so careful. There was . . . bad luck. Health stuff. You know."

I nodded, but of course I didn't know.

"Anyway, it should have been more like this. It should have been exactly like this." Even as I sat there blowing the foam out my nose and into a napkin, his eyes let me know that he was talking about me, that I was fun, someone he wished he'd known before now.

“Just promise me one thing, Beautiful Brianna,” Derek said, pulling a couple of bucks out of his pocket for a tip. “Promise me you won’t ever make big, life-changing decisions just because you’re afraid of the unknown.”

“Um, okay,” I said, laughing a little.

Derek stared at me again, that calm, barely-there smile on his face. “God, you’re something else.”

We drove around some more after leaving the coffeehouse; of course nobody cared if I was out that late. When he drove me home, we sat in the car in front of Keisha’s house for a long time, sometimes talking, sometimes not.

Then he said, “I’ve never met anyone like you. You’re so smart and funny. You’re one of the lucky ones.”

I snorted a little at that last part, but Derek just looked at me for a second, his face all serious. Then he said, “How could you be unlucky? I mean, look at you. You have everything. The guys must go wild.”

Which was the thing that finally pushed me right over the edge and into oblivion, because nobody had actually told me that in quite the same way before.

So I let him kiss me. Or maybe he let me kiss him. All I know is, his lips were on mine and I was arching my back, trying to get closer.

And let me just stop here and say I know what most people would be thinking at this point. A married man = ew. Especially for a girl who’s only sixteen (and a half). But as I said before, I had no idea Derek was married. And yes, I should have done my research first. But there was no wedding ring on his finger, and things were happening so fast and the whole thing was so surreal. The truth was I didn’t think long enough about it to ask.

After we kissed in front of Keisha’s house for a while, he whispered in this breathy voice, “I’ll walk you to the door. It’s dark.”

We kissed some more on the doorstep, and he said, "This is the part where you're supposed to invite me inside. If you want to, I mean."

"Well, you're obviously not going to leave me alone anytime soon," I said, smiling my best vixen smile. "Plus, my roommates are out of town."

The kissing continued once we were in the hallway, but it was more intense, with me pressing against him as hard as I could. Derek didn't resist, but he didn't try to take advantage, either. I wasn't being ignored like in junior high, and I was wasn't pushing my vixen moves on someone who wasn't ready, someone I'd eventually hurt. Even better, I didn't feel like a girl getting her picture taken while she slept or being groped by a creep in her sister's kitchen. I responded to this feeling by loosening his belt and unbuttoning his khakis as I pulled him toward the laundry room. Once we were lying together on my bed, I could see the signpost up ahead in my brain, the one that read YOU KNOW WHERE THIS ROAD LEADS. And we blew right past it. We were both naked from the waist down, still kissing, his breath louder than it had been just seconds before and his heart pounding like crazy against my chest.

"Are we . . . covered?" he asked.

And because I didn't get that he was talking about birth control—because, stupidly, birth control was the last thing on my mind—I looked at the bedsheet in a moment of confusion. "Of course," I said, pulling it up over us. "Of course we are."

Afterward, we lay there in silence for a few minutes, Derek's heart still going *thumpa-thumpa,* and I wondered if he was being quiet because he thought I'd been a virgin or something. When he rolled off me and onto his side, more silence followed, until I started to wonder if maybe he was mad about something.

But then he sat up and shook his head, not looking at me. "What the hell am I doing?" he asked, but it seemed hypothetical.

I tried to think of an answer anyway as Derek scooted to the edge of the bed, tugging the sheet away from me a little. I pulled the sheet back over myself as I watched him stand up. His shirt was wrinkled and damp, covering everything above the crease where his butt met his thighs, and his quads flexed a little as he started to take a step toward the kitchen. I thought about saying something casual, something like *You have really awesome legs,* but all of a sudden he seemed to be frozen in place except for one of his hands, which rose up toward his chest and covered his heart like he was about to recite the Pledge of Allegiance.

When he went down it was in slow motion, collapsing from the knees first, and then the rest of his body following until his head made that *thwack* sound against the edge of the bedside table.

7

jailbait

KEISHA AND ROBBY are back from their weekend in Sedona when I get home from school on the Monday of Derek's flagpole memorial. Both of them have taken the day off work, and Robby is out with his friends.

As soon as I walk through the door and put my backpack down on a kitchen chair, Keisha corners me. She got home a second before I did, and she still has a bag of groceries in her arms. She doesn't say hello, doesn't ask how my weekend went. Instead, she simply says in a slow, quiet voice, "Jennifer from next door told me an ambulance was here the other night. She also said the police showed up." Because that's Keisha's way—dead calm before the sky opens up and all hell breaks loose.

Considering everything that's happened since Friday night, all I can think to say in reply is "Something went down here this weekend, Keish, and I'm really bent about it. So don't be getting on my case right now, okay?"

I'm surprised by my ability to play it so cool, but Keisha just puts down the groceries and looks at me over the top of her fake Bulgari sunglasses—the ones she got from a street vendor in

Phoenix. They look real, with little rhinestones at the corners of the frames and everything. "Say what?" she says.

"Okay, yes," I tell her, backpedaling a little because I don't want her totally going off on me. "There were paramedics here, okay?"

"Paramedics," Keisha repeats, ever so slowly. "In my house." Her voice has gotten pretornado calm. "You're telling me there were paramedics here."

"Yes, Keish," I say. "But I'm also telling you not to freak out about it. Did you even hear that part?" I try throwing a little attitude into my voice again, but I'm not as good at it as Keisha is. So I end up telling her the whole story—minus the details like Derek's age and the fact that his wife is my English teacher—because everything is already way more messed up and confusing than it needs to be. When I'm done explaining, it occurs to me that I may have stunned my sister for the first time in her life, because, mercifully, she has nothing more to say and no more questions to ask.

I take advantage of her shock and disappear into my room. I'm still in there when Robby comes home later that night, and I can tell right away Keisha is reporting what happened, giving him her version of the story, because her voice is really quiet. It's just a murmur, really, and I can't even begin to make out the words, even though the kitchen is right next to my room.

Then I hear Robby say, "No shit?" and start laughing his head off, which is about the kind of reaction I'd expect from him. I have no idea why Keisha is so desperate to hang on to Robby, other than because "We look so hot together, Bree. It's incredible," which she told me once. I didn't say anything at the time, just turned my head fast and fake-sneezed so she wouldn't see me laughing.

Robby also takes the next day, Tuesday, off work. Turns out

he's going to take Wednesday, Thursday, and Friday off, too, because the construction yard where he's been employed for just over a month has started to kill his soul. After Keisha leaves for her job at the Stop'n'Shop, he loiters in the kitchen while I clean up the dishes.

"I've heard all about it, you know," he says. "And not just from Keisha. I know people who saw you girls sucking some dude's neck at the Frog Friday night."

"Well, good for you," I say, not bothering to clarify that it was Jules who kissed Derek's neck at the Frog. "You actually know people. What do you want, a gold star sticker or something?"

"Funny, Brianna," Robby laughs, but it sounds like he's been sucking on lemons. "You're funny. You know that?" Somehow it's not as charming coming from him as it was coming from Derek on Friday night. "But here's the thing. There are words for girls like you—underage girls who sleep with grown men. Girls who skank around with other women's husbands."

"As usual, you don't know what the hell you're talking about," I say. Even as I say it, though, a cold sweat breaks out along my spine. Because I know he's right. There *are* words for girls like me.

The next thing I know, Robby is stepping closer to me and saying, "I know exactly what I'm talking about, jailbait."

I can't think of a single thing to say or do, so I just stand there remembering how my seventh-grade English teacher told us that when we were trying to describe something, we should always think *TTHSS* (sounds like "this"), for Taste, Touch, Hear, See, Smell. That way, we could use the five senses in our description. Of course, one of the boys at the back of the room said under his breath, "Or you could think *SSHTT*," and everyone just lost it.

So, here's the SSHTT version of what happens when Robby

comes close: First, I *smell* his aftershave and I *see* his face getting red, almost like he's blushing but more like he's mad. Then I *hear* him clear his throat. I'm not sure why he does this, because it's not like he's saying anything. I *taste* a little fear as I look down at the steak knife I was about to wash before Robby started shooting his mouth off. I want to keep an eye on it just in case something scares me and I accidentally stab one of us. That thought makes me laugh (which Robby takes as an invitation to come even closer, so that we're practically wearing each other's clothes). He raises one hand like he's going to *touch* my head, but instead he gathers my hair in a fist and lifts it up in one quick move. His slobbery mouth is on the back of my neck so fast I don't even have time to think about stabbing anyone. I simply freeze. Then I say the first thing that pops into my brain, which is "Get the hell away from me, asshole."

Robby looks at me in surprise for a second and then laughs again. "You're shaping up to be a real tease, you know that?" But he takes a step back when I grab the knife and hold it up.

Later that night I'm lying in bed, completely tense and feeling as alone as I've ever felt in my life. I can hear Robby and Keisha fighting in their room, and a white-hot flash of fear shoots through me at the thought of Robby leaking the story of what happened between us in the kitchen this morning. I can't make out the words of their argument, though, and when it sounds like things have settled down, I fall into a nervous, jumpy kind of sleep.

I wake up with a jolt just before midnight, and it's not because of a nightmare or a loud sound. I wake up because Keisha is standing over my bed like the Bride of Chucky, looking down at me with eyes full of 100 percent honest-to-goodness crazy.

"Really, Bree?" she's saying. "*Really?* Messing around with *my* man in *my* house?"

What the hell is she talking about? Me messing around with loser penguin freak Robby? I try to blink the sleep out of my eyes and look at my sister's hands, just to make sure she doesn't have a baseball bat or an Uzi. Then I think I go, "Whaaa?" because thoughts are moving through my brain at the speed of frozen honey. There's no time to say more, because the next thing I know Keisha is yanking one of my sweatshirts from the dirty clothes hamper, throwing it at my face, and screaming, "Out of my house! *Now!*"

And knowing what I know about Keisha, I do what she says.

Once I'm up and stumbling around, trying to gather my most important stuff, the brain fog clears off a little, and the pieces start falling into place. I suddenly get that Robby must have thought I was going to tell Keisha what he did at breakfast. He must have decided to get to her first and cover his ass by "confessing" everything that happened between him and me in the kitchen. Only, he had to have put his own little spin on it—making it sound like I was the one who came on to him rather than the other way around. And Keisha being Keisha, of course she'd believe Robby's story over mine. Because I may be her blood relative, but he's the one who keeps her from being alone at night, who lets her be the boss and keeps her warm with his smiley penguins and his BS (there's no way I'd say it out loud, but it's like Keisha and Jolene are the same person at this moment).

Robby's standing in their doorway when I get to the hall, and it surprises me to see that even he looks a little freaked out by Keisha's reaction. I'm even more surprised when he starts trying to talk her down.

"Take it easy, Keish," he says. "This is ridiculous."

But she shoots him a look with the potential to vaporize him right there on the spot, and he looks away like a kicked dog.

Seconds later I'm standing out on their front lawn, still pulling the sweatshirt down over my pajamas with a bunch of my stuff strewn about me—stuff Keisha threw outside after she kicked my butt out the door. When I look back at the front step, my sister is standing there with her arms crossed over her chest.

"One strike, Brianna," she says in the flattest voice possible.

"I'm out." I finish the sentence for her and bend down to gather my clothes. "I know."

Then the front door slams, and I'm alone for real, doing my best to start forgetting everything I thought I knew about sisterly loyalty. I know Keisha isn't going to cool down anytime soon, and there's no way Robby's going to be able to talk her out of it. Here's the thing: if he's smart (which he isn't), he'll stay as far away from her as possible, because if I know my sister (and I do), Robby just might be the next member of the household standing out here on the lawn, half dressed and wondering what the hell just happened. For a split second I consider camping out in front of the house for the night—just piling a bunch of my clothes together in a kind of nest and getting more sleep until I can figure out what to do in the morning. But then the front door opens and Keisha sticks her head out. "Don't you even *think* about staying around here," she says in that dead-calm voice of hers. I guess she knows me as well as I know her.

So here's what I do: I pile as many of my clothes together as I can and stash them near one of the raggedy hedges that run across the front of the house. I pluck a few pairs of underwear from the pile and cram them and some T-shirts inside my backpack before carefully folding all the other stuff, because I hate a mess. That's ironic, I guess, since I seem to have endless talent for making a complete mess of my life.

And then I start walking. My oversized pajama top is balled up under my sweatshirt in a way that makes it look like I'm about to give birth, but rather than worry about it I just keep walking (even though I don't have a clue where I'm going). As I walk I remember something Derek said to me the night we met: "You are a unique girl. A unique, slightly unmoored girl."

He said it while I sat across from him at the coffeehouse, sketching his face, and I must have given him a blank look, because then he said, "Unmoored means untethered. It's like... unattached to anything. It can also mean unhinged, like—"

"I know what it means," I told him, even though I didn't.

Because I can't think of anywhere else to go, I decide to walk to Jules's house, which is about a mile away from Keisha and Robby's. Twenty minutes later, I'm there, standing on the sidewalk looking up at her bedroom window. Jules lives in an attic above her parents' garage, which is cool because it's almost like her own little apartment. But to get to it you have to go through the house. As exhausted as I am, I still don't want to wake anybody up at this hour, so I don't ring the bell. Instead, I sit down on the front step and close my eyes, pulling my arms inside my sweatshirt and curling into a ball to keep warm.

8

slut city

THAT'S WHERE I am a few hours later, at sunrise, when Jules's father comes outside to get the newspaper and nearly steps on me.

"Holy—" he says, startling me awake. His eyes are huge, which I guess is understandable: it's not every day a guy wakes up to find a homeless cheerleader with posttraumatic stress disorder asleep on his front step.

"I'm here to see Jules," I tell him.

"Uh, okay," he says. "Come on in, then." He doesn't sound so sure, though, and he watches me carefully as I stand up, push my arms back through the sleeves of my sweatshirt, and then reach up to check my hair. Naturally, it's sticking out from my head at all sorts of crazy angles, adding yet another detail to the portrait of complete wreckage that is Brianna Taylor.

Upstairs in her bedroom Jules is still asleep. She looks different without her makeup and her attitude, almost childlike with most of her face smooshed into the pillow. She must sense me standing there, though, because she wakes up and looks right at me with one eye. "The hell," she mutters, slurping a little line of drool back into her mouth.

"Keisha kicked me out."

That's all it takes to make her sit up fast, because, as I said, nobody likes a juicy story more than Jules. "Oh my God, Bree."

I don't go to school that day. Jules's mom, who is a lawyer and who looks like she just stepped out of *Vogue* magazine, clearly doesn't quite understand what's going on. As we're all standing downstairs in the kitchen a little while later—me, Jules, and her parents—I can hear by Mrs. Hill's voice that she's not at all thrilled about the idea of me staying in their house by myself.

But then Jules tells her, "God, Mom. It's not like Brianna's planning to host an orgy here or anything. I mean, look at her. She looks like she hasn't slept in a week. Would you make *me* go to school looking like that?"

Jules has never tried to hide the fact that she thinks her parents are complete idiots, and this isn't the first time I've wanted to remind her how lucky she is to have parents who care, even though I'm sure it's kind of a pain to be told when to wake up, what to eat, and when to be home. Jules probably sees being parentless as some sort of awesome freedom. When we're in her room with the door closed I say, "Dude, you're so harsh with your mom and dad."

"Yeah, whatever," she snorts. Then, out of nowhere, she says, "Do you even know how much money they spent on fertility treatments and then a surrogate just so they could have a kid?"

"I guess they really wanted you."

"Are you serious? What they 'wanted,'" she says, her fingers making air quotes, "was to have a little trophy daughter they could parade around to show how well they were keeping up with the Joneses—all their friends who were having perfect little children, too. That's basically what I am. A trophy. Just another high-priced object to show everyone what a smashing success their lives turned out to be. 'Anything less than excellence means you're not trying hard enough,'" she says, again with the air quotes. "Well, screw that. Screw them and their 'expectations.' I'm not a golden goddamn statue."

I've never heard anything like this from Jules, and so I just stand there in silence. For the first time ever, I see a vulnerable side of her, even though she switches right back into tough girl mode. I guess I thought she was immune from feeling less than perfect, because she pretty much acts as if she owns the world 100 percent of the time. "I'm really sorry, Jules," I say after a while.

"What? Oh, please. Seriously. Shut the hell up," she says. "As if I care what my parents think. They're freaks, but they're just so easy to mess with. I mean, what would the neighbors think if I went totally off the rails? I guess I like to keep them on their toes. If nothing else, it keeps me sane when they're out there trying to pretend that everyone in my family poops rainbows."

Jules manages to convince her mother that I can be safely left in their house for the day, but as they walk out the front door, Mrs. Hill still doesn't look so sure. I'm glad Jules is able to bully her parents so well, though, because after they're gone, I wander through their spotless rooms and look at all their things. It's not like I'm a klepto or anything, but sometimes seeing the way other people live can be just as thrilling as being in on a secret.

There are pictures of Jules as a toddler with pigtails, of the three of them on vacation, of the three of them in a formal Christmas pose. I look through their medicine cabinets and find Band-Aids and pill bottles, prescriptions for antianxiety drugs that I recognize from TV commercials—"Because It's Good to Be Happy." I walk into Mr. and Mrs. Hill's bedroom and start going through stuff there, touching things lightly. Jules's father keeps a gun in the top drawer of his bedside table. There's a bowl full of coins and a wad of cash there, too. And all of a sudden I realize what I'm trying to do: I'm trying to figure out what normal looks like.

It's clear from the way Mrs. Hill acted that staying here isn't going to be a permanent solution, so after I'm done snooping around the house I grab a pad of paper and a pen from the kitchen drawer. Then I sit down on the family room couch and make a list of other possibilities. After ten minutes, though, this is all I come up with:

1. Get Keisha to forgive me (fat chance).
2. Sell my body so I can afford to rent a place of my own (ha ha, but still more realistic than #1).
3. Get Jolene to let me come back home.

That last one is almost as much of a long shot as the first, but I pick up the phone anyway. Jolene answers, and when I ask her if I can stay with her and Larry for a while, it takes her exactly half a second to say no.

"Guests and fish have one thing in common, Brianna," she laughs. "Do you know what that is?"

"No," I say.

"They both start to stink after a few days."

Which I guess is her way of saying that having me there would be like having rotting seafood in the house. Nice.

"I have nowhere else to go," I tell her.

"You and Keisha will work it out," she says. "Just bring her a cute piece of jewelry or something."

"Right," I say before hanging up. "That's a great idea."

I'm upstairs in Jules's room when she gets home from school a couple of hours later. "You won't be*lieve* who was already back at school today," she says, closing the door behind her and dropping her backpack next to the bed.

"Plain Jane," I say, my voice unenthusiastic.

"Right! And when she took roll and called your name and you weren't there, there was this *total* awkward silence. I mean, I don't think anybody in that room was daring to even *breathe*."

My blood runs cold. "Why?" I ask. "It's not like anybody knows about what happened."

The smile fades from Jules's face.

"Right?" I ask her, my voice louder now.

I can tell she's trying to figure out a way to change the subject. "No," she says. "But it's just weird not having you there, you know?"

Which makes exactly zero sense, but I decide to let her off the hook. "Whatever." I sense something in the air, though, and I have a sudden suspicion that Jules is getting too wrapped up in her juiciest story yet—a story with me as the bad guy.

At dinner that night, Mrs. Hill still looks like she doesn't quite trust me, so I just try to smile at her a lot and offer to help with the dishes after Jules goes up to her room. It softens Mrs. Hill a little, but I can tell she's still uncomfortable. After I finish filling the dishwasher I say, "Thanks again for letting me stay here. It really means a lot."

"Mmhm," she says, raising her eyebrows but not looking at me, which is clearly my cue to leave her alone.

The stairs to Jules's room are carpeted, which means she can't hear me heading up there. When I step into the room, she's on her cell phone with her head turned the other way, so she doesn't see me, either.

"No *way*, Brade," she says, and I can tell by the giggling that she's talking to Braden Lewis, that she's in red-hot gossip mode yet again. It makes me smile to hear her voice so animated.

"I know," Jules continues, lowering her voice a little. "Bree just got totally out of control."

I freeze, not sure if I'm really hearing what I think I'm hearing.

"Total Slut City," Jules continues, still unaware that I'm standing right there—and that's when I even startle myself a little.

"You have got to be kidding me," I say, my voice loud and sharp enough to make Jules drop the phone. She picks it up fast, though, and whips her head around, her face once again that of a little girl. This time, though, she looks like a little girl who's just been caught swiping frosting off a cake.

"I gotta go," she tells Braden, and ends the call. Then, obviously trying to make it look like nothing out of the ordinary has happened, she gives me a defiant look and says, "What?"

"You just completely threw me under the bus."

Jules's eyes start darting around, but then she blinks and looks right at me. "Actually, Bree, you threw yourself under the bus."

"What the hell is that supposed to mean?"

"It means you had your fun torturing Mrs. Playne and everything, but I really think you took it too far."

"*My* fun?" My voice is louder than I mean for it to be. "*My* fun? What about your fun? You came up with, like, ninety-nine percent of the ideas for torturing her. Plus, you know I had no clue who Derek was that night. None of us did!" And then I remember the look in Jules's eyes when Derek and I left the Frog together; it was the forced smile of a first runner-up, and I knew at the time that somehow I'd pay for taking what Jules had claimed for herself when she kissed the back of Derek's neck.

"Anyway," she says, like we're now having a friendly chat. "I just never thought you'd sink so low as to actually go after someone's husband."

"But none of us knew—" I try to explain again.

"It's, like, totally against every basic Girl 101 rule there is. And . . . I don't know. Maybe you should just leave."

That last part slips out so naturally, with such easy cruelty, that it makes me wish she'd just stood up and slapped me across the face instead.

I stand there, speechless, for what feels like forever, and then, when tears start rising up in my eyes, I reach for my backpack. There's no way I'm going to give her the satisfaction of seeing me cry. Most of the stuff I brought is still in there, so I turn around and walk out of the room, down the carpeted stairs, and through the front door. Mrs. Hill's voice calls after me from the living room—"Jules? Is that you?"—but I don't bother answering.

I stand in front of the Hills' house for a minute, wiping my eyes with back of my sleeve and trying to get my bearings. The last thing I see before I start walking again is Jules's mom framed in the window of their family room, watching me. She moves away from the window when she sees me watching *her,* but she doesn't go to the front door and open it. She doesn't come outside and try to convince me to stay.

9

boom

THE HILLS' HOUSE is only a block from where downtown starts, and I go inside the first place I find that's open. As soon as I'm sitting in a booth, I realize it's the same coffeehouse where Derek drew the smiley-face portrait of me on a napkin. It's where he told me I was beautiful and unmoored. I have three dollars and some change in my pocket, and I use most of it to buy myself a cup of coffee and some time. I wonder for a second if I should find a pay phone and see if Coach Kristy would let me stay with her, but then I decide that would be completely awkward. Once the coffee's gone and I'm feeling too jittery to sit in the booth for one more second, I head back out.

I end up at the public library, which is the only other place I can think of where I won't look like a freak for wandering around without purpose. It's almost eight o'clock when I get there, though, so I barely have any time to sit in one of the big reading chairs and think about my next move before the librarian calls out that they'll be closing in five minutes.

Once they do close, I stand out front and watch the other library patrons head toward their cars and their bikes. I stand there until the librarian herself comes out and locks the doors from the outside. She smiles at me as she walks past.

"Have a good night," she says.

"You too." I wonder what she would do if I asked her for money, or if I asked her for a ride—but to where? I could probably go to Charlotte's or Kimmy's, but who knows what Jules has told them by now?

Earlier this year, a bunch of people in town raised money to have a fancy wooden footbridge built over the creek behind the library, and that's where I finally decide to go after the librarian gets into her car and drives away, waving to me one last time before leaving the parking lot empty. The creek is dried up now, and I have to climb down an embankment to get underneath the bridge. I mutter to myself as I pull my backpack in after me and settle in: "This is great, Bree. Real classy. And you thought Keisha's laundry room was cramped."

There could be worse places to sit and think, though. Early September is beautiful in northern Arizona, with the aspen leaves whispering up on the Peaks and armies of sunflowers nodding their heads along every roadside. As I pull my arms back into the sweatshirt for yet another attempt at outdoor sleep, it occurs to me that there's something peaceful about having this little bit of public space all to myself. But then the dark brings with it an unexpected cold, and while the night wears on I keep thinking I hear footsteps and voices nearby. I start wondering if anyone would hear me if I screamed for help. This thought keeps me awake for what feels like hours, until my eyelids won't stay open any longer, and all sounds dissolve into a restless sleep.

I wake up at dawn with every muscle in my body sore from sleeping tense and cold and curled up in a sitting position. There's not enough room under the bridge to stretch, and I also have to pee, which means it's time to head back out to who-knows-where. When I reach for my backpack, I see that a piece of paper has been tucked underneath, which means someone *was* here and I slept right through it. That thought makes me shiver more than the cold morning air, until I unfold the paper and read what it says. There's a picture of a woman cradling a young child, and above it are an address, a phone number, and the words HOMELESS? HOPELESS? CHECK OUT HOPE HOUSE, A SAFE HAVEN FOR WOMEN. Without even pausing to think about it, I crawl out from under the bridge, grab the backpack, and start walking.

The shelter is only two blocks away, and I hold the flyer in my hand as I walk, in case they want to see it. Then I realize how stupid this is. It's not like it's a movie theater and I need a ticket to get in. "Stupid," I call myself under my breath as I hitch my backpack higher up so it will stop rubbing in the same spot with every step I take.

There's a metal fence around the property, and there's a speaker box near the gate like they have at fast-food drive-thrus. A red button on the box has a sign below it that says PUSH FOR ENTRY, so that's what I do.

"Help you?" a female voice crackles back at me.

I resist the urge to order a double cheeseburger and instead say, "My name is Emily, I'm eighteen, and I have nowhere else to go." I know better than to give them my real name or my real age, since either one could land me in foster care. Which is so not an option. I've already thought ahead enough on the walk over here to the point where, if they ask me for my birth certificate or any other identifying information, I'll just say I had to leave it behind when I fled my house. And I also plan to tell them I'm taking classes at the community college. Paranoid, maybe, but I'm not taking any chances.

"Buzzing you through," the voice says. "Close the gate tight behind you."

I have to walk through sort of an outdoor alleyway-type thing before I get to the front door, but once inside I can see it's just like a normal house other than the reception area set up in one corner. A young woman with black hair and eyes so dark they look black, too, is sitting behind a desk there, and she watches me come in.

"You the bridge girl?"

"Excuse me?"

"One of my volunteers called in. Said there was a young girl sleeping under the bridge behind the library, and he left a flyer under her stuff. That you?"

"I'm not that young," I say, trying to look her right in the eye without wavering. "I take classes at the community college."

"Yeah, okay," she says, smiling. "Whatever. What did you say your name was?"

"Emily."

"You got any drugs on you?" she asks.

"Pardon?"

"Look," she says. "We're here to help girls like you, but we're not stupid. If you're on anything or in possession, feel free to turn around and walk right back out that door."

"No drugs," I tell her, wondering what I've gotten myself into.

"Any kids?"

"God, no."

"Are you fleeing physical or emotional abuse of any kind? Someone who's violent?"

"Aren't these questions a little personal?"

She stops and looks at me. "Yes. They are."

I don't answer her for a second. If I tell her I'm not running away from anyone, maybe she won't let me stay here. But I know it would feel wrong on a deeper level than I'm ready to deal with to lie about something like this, so I say, "No. No abuse. I just don't have anywhere else to go right now."

"All right," she says, nodding. Then she holds out her hand, and I shake it. "I'm Monique, by the way. You can call me Mo."

"Okay."

"So here's the deal... Emily." She says the name I've given her in a way that makes me think she's on to me. "Basically, you get seven days here, no questions asked—as long as you're looking for work and helping out around the place. After that, if you want to stay longer, we'll need to see documentation of your age, the classes you're taking... stuff like that."

Mo turns to reach for a photocopy of the house rules on a little table behind her, and I notice two teardrops tattooed on the side of her neck with fancy cursive writing beneath each one. When she turns back around, she catches me staring. It seems to make her impatient. "That one is for my little boy," she says, pointing to the top teardrop. "He died before he was born."

"Oh," I tell her. "I'm so sorry."

She waves her hand—like she's flicking my apology away—and continues. "I was pregnant, and Tony—his father—got wasted and mad one night. Kicked me in the stomach. I hemorrhaged. End of story."

"I don't even know what to—"

"And that one," she says, ignoring me and pointing at the second teardrop tattoo, which is empty at the top but filled in with black ink at the bottom. "That one's for Tony. He's dead now, too."

"Oh." I wonder if she had anything to do with it.

"I can tell you this, Emily," Mo says like she's reading my thoughts. "There's always a price to pay."

"I'll remember that," I tell her.

A few other women are wandering the halls as Mo shows me to my tiny bedroom and tells me I still have time to eat breakfast if I hurry. "After that," she says, "you have to be out of here until three. That's when we open back up. Sign out anytime you leave, then sign back in when you return. Curfew's at nine p.m., so no coming back for the night after that. Try to bring drugs or a man in here and you're out. I think I already told you that. Also, you have to sign up for the chores list. Pick something you're good at. Or at least something you don't totally hate."

It's probably a good thing they have all these rules, because I can tell right away the shelter is bare-bones and understaffed, and it's pretty clear just about any psycho ex-husband or boyfriend could easily blast in here with a rifle and do away with everyone if he wanted to. I try to tell myself this is just temporary, that I'm at camp or a sleepover at a new friend's house, like I tried to do when Keisha and I were placed in the CPS dorms. Myself is too old to fall for that line anymore, though; I know where I am, and it sure isn't camp.

Lately I've been remembering someone else from those weeks in the CPS dorm, too—a guest speaker lady who came during the month Keisha and I were there. She was an adult, and I'm not sure I ever knew her name, but she'd been in the system herself. I remember her sitting in front of all of us during Group and making us promise we wouldn't let our experiences up to that point define us, that we had to figure out ways to add them to our "life toolboxes" and turn them into something positive.

"Because very few people have the kinds of experiences all of you in this room have had," she said, looking around at each of us. When she got to me her eyes seemed to pause for a second. "And, believe it or not, that makes you pretty special. It might even make you brave, if you let it." At the time, I thought I was tuning her out, but something about being here at Hope House makes me realize I was listening more than I thought.

I look like such a train wreck from sleeping under the library bridge that I don't dare go to school. Instead, when all the residents sign out after breakfast, I go back to the bridge for a nap. This looks like it's going to work pretty well until a couple of burnouts not much older than me show up and say, "Man, we got squatters' rights here."

"Fine," I tell them, crawling back out into the sunshine and wondering where they were last night.

"Got any weed?" they ask as I'm walking away, but I don't even bother answering.

I spend the day wandering around downtown, looking at window displays and avoiding going back to Keisha and Robby's house to see about the clothes I left by the bushes. As soon as Hope House opens back up that afternoon, I'm there. After cleaning the mirrors in the bathroom (which was one of the chores I signed up for), I go straight to bed, where I stare up at the ceiling for a few minutes before falling into a fast, hard sleep.

I sleep right through dinner, and in the middle of the night, I hear a child's voice cry out in the room next to mine—"I want Daddy!" Then I hear a woman's voice soothing him. For a minute, I don't know where I am, but then I remember and fall back asleep. I dream about the moon falling out of the sky: big fireball, big explosion. Boom, world in darkness.

I meet my hall mates the next morning in the combined kitchen–dining area, where a few basic things like cereal, fruit, and English muffins have been set out on the counter by that day's breakfast volunteer. I'm sitting alone in a folding metal chair with my bowl of generic oat Os when a woman walks in and starts putting some things on a plate. She's wearing a huge yellow T-shirt that says PARADISE PLUMBING across the front, and she glances over at me. "I'm Angie," she says. "I hope the kids and I didn't keep you up last night."

"You didn't," I tell her.

Angie comes over to the table and pulls out a chair by the window. Then she seems to think better of it and chooses one next to the wall. After talking with her for a while, I learn she had to escape her house in the middle of the night when her husband threatened to shoot her and she was too scared to call the police.

"I don't even know whose clothes we're wearing," Angie says, giving the T-shirt a little tug. "But it's hardest on my kids, Sam and Laurel. They don't understand any of it."

"Where are they?" I ask.

"Mo's watching them outside so I can have a few minutes."

"It's too bad there's not more stuff for them to do here."

"They're understaffed and underfunded," she says, shrugging. "But thank God for people like Mo."

"She's pretty tough," I say.

"She has to be if she's going to keep running this place for the county without enough resources to even hire decent help. Gotta hand it to her, though. At least she chooses being here and helping where she can over her old gang life."

"I hadn't thought of it that way."

"Well, Emily, that's one of the benefits of getting old," Angie says, laughing. "You get to start thinking about things differently."

"You're so not old."

"I don't know," she says, sighing and standing up to clear her plate. "Sometimes lately I feel like I'm about a thousand."

After Angie leaves, I eat the rest of my Os in silence, staring down at my bowl. I do glance up once, though, to see Sam and Laurel, who have come around to this side of the building and settled into a block of sunlight just outside the window. When they see me smiling at them, they stop what they're doing and wave.

10

tea and crumpets

I STAY AWAY from school that entire week. It's not like Jolene is going to have a clue where I am if they call to tell her I haven't been showing up. Plus, I need some time to get my head together and figure out a game plan.

I offer to do more around the shelter when I see Mo is particularly busy. At first, she shrugs off my offers, but after I've gone above and beyond for a couple of days, she stops me in the hall and says, "Thanks, Emily." She even gives me an old duffel bag left behind by one of the previous residents so I can go by Keisha's place when she's at work and get the rest of my stuff, which is, miraculously, still hidden in the bushes.

After signing out of Hope House each morning, I head downtown to look for Help Wanted signs. I catch my reflection as I walk past the big storefront windows. My hair is wild and I'm not wearing makeup. I hardly recognize myself. As long as I say I've been out looking for a job or taking my classes at the community college, Hope House gives me fifteen dollars a day to live on. I feel a little bad about taking the money, but I don't know what else to do. Also, I know Mo is going to start expecting results, like an actual job offer or that "documentation" from the CC, before too much longer.

Those are the things I'm worrying about on my sixth night at the shelter when I overhear women's voices in the hallway as I'm heading toward the kitchen. Of course, women's voices are nothing new here. What is new is that one of the voices is familiar, and it's saying my name—my real one, not Emily.

"I'm looking for a girl named Brianna Taylor," the familiar voice says. "Do you have a girl by that name staying here?"

The second voice is Mo's. "I'm sorry, but I'm not able to divulge this kind of information about our residents."

But then the other woman catches sight of me as I round the corner and we nearly come face to face. "Brianna?"

I recognize her the same way I recognized her when she came barreling through the doors of the emergency room. And I think the same thing, too: *Oh, crap.*

She's wearing another one of her infinite scarves, like she was that night, and one look at Plain Jane is all it takes to spin me around and send me fast in the opposite direction. I speed-walk down the hall, away from her and toward my room—once again, much like the night Derek died, when I fled across the ER parking lot and back toward Keisha's car—back toward escape—as fast as my legs could carry me.

This time, though, Plain Jane's voice follows me: "The school's been looking for you," she calls out, loudly enough for some other residents to poke their heads out into the hall to see what's going on. "You haven't been in class all week, Brianna. That's called truancy."

I guess I really think at that moment that if I just keep moving, she'll go away, that all of it will just go away. But then Plain Jane says the next thing, the thing that stops me in my tracks:

"You can't just keep running."

I turn around and glare at her like, *Why the hell not?* Then I glare at Mo, who's standing there looking like a couple of three-headed showgirls have just landed in the hallway of Hope House.

"Why did you let her in here?" I demand.

"Excuse me?" Mo says, and it's spooky how much she reminds me of Keisha at that moment. "When women show up at the gate and say it's an emergency, we let them in." She looks at Plain Jane and then looks at me."Do you know this woman, Emily?"

For a second I think about lying and telling her I've never seen Derek's wife in my life.

But then Plain Jane has to go and say, "Emily? Who's Emily?"

"Yeah, I know her," I tell Mo.

"I'm her teacher," Plain Jane adds.

"From the community college?" Mo asks her.

Plain Jane just looks at me.

"I'll let you two have a moment," Mo says, and walks back down the hall toward her desk. Before she does, though, her eyes land on mine in a way that says, *You lied, and I'm pissed.*

"Can you blame me for asking around?" Plain Jane says when we're standing there alone again. "I am your teacher, you know. And the truth is, Brianna, from what I can tell, it doesn't sound like anyone else is rushing to help you right now."

"Who says I need help?" I can feel my lower jaw jutting out with stupid pride when I say this, but I don't even care. How dare she come in here like some kind of wannabe superhero on a mission to save the poor homeless girl? Instead of saying this to her, though, I just say, "God, I don't even want to know what they're saying about me on the squad."

"You've got to be kidding me," Plain Jane says, and it's the first time I can remember hearing anything like sarcasm coming out of her mouth. "That's what you're worried about?" She looks around and lowers her voice. "I mean, you've been sleeping in a battered *women's* shelter for the past week and you're worried about what the other high school *cheerleaders* are saying about you?"

She has a point. But cheer is the main thing that has kept me feeling at least sort of normal the whole time I've been in high school, and I am thinking about it. I'm starting to regret not showing up at school at all this week, because I've also missed two practices. One more and I'm off the squad. "Call me shallow," I tell my English teacher, "I really don't care."

But Plain Jane's face has changed, and it clearly isn't easy for her to say the next thing she says. "Brianna, I want to tell you something else. I feel partially responsible for what happened."

Since I don't even know how to begin to respond to that, I just say, "So what is it you want, exactly?"

Plain Jane takes a deep breath, then lets it out. "I want you to come home with me," she says. "I know you don't have anywhere else to go."

And I'm about to just stand there and laugh right in her face. I'm about to say, "Seriously? You have got to be kidding me."

But the truth is, she's right, and I know my lies have finally caught up with me. As if to prove it, Mo appears in the hallway again right at that moment. She looks first at Plain Jane and then at me, and I know she's heard everything. "You know the drill, Emily. Or Brianna. Or whoever you are," she says. "I need to see documentation—some proof of age. Now."

Fortunately, I don't have a lot of stuff to gather up. After closing the door of my room, I poke my head into Angie's room and say good-bye to her and the kids. All three of them are sitting on Angie's bed laughing about something, and they look surprised when I tell them I'm leaving.

"Are you coming back?" Laurel asks as her mom comes to the doorway to give me a hug.

I shake my head. "See you," I tell Angie.

Back in the reception area, I sign out of Hope House one last time (not really necessary, I guess, but it feels like the right thing to do) and follow my English teacher through the iron gate and out to her car. It's the same car Derek was driving the night he took me back to Keisha's house, and it still smells the same inside—like leather and soap. Sitting in that car makes me feel like a trapped animal, and I'm pretty sure Plain Jane is enjoying it.

My face is getting tired from being held in a scowl, and right when I think I might start to die inside from the awkward silence, Plain Jane decides to speak up.

"He had a bad heart," she says.

"Excuse me?" I know what she said, but I have no clue how to answer her.

And she must think I'm a full-on idiot, because she sighs and tries to clarify for me. "Derek? Derek Playne?" Her voice is higher-pitched all of a sudden, and I start to wonder if it was a mistake getting into the car with her. "My husband? I believe you two met."

I glance at her hands, which are gripping the steering wheel like she wants to squish it to death. Her fingernails are a nightmare—gnawed down to the quick, with ratty cuticles and, of course, no polish whatsoever. "I'm sorry," she says, taking a deep breath and then letting it out. "I told myself I wasn't going to come unhinged like that."

"It's okay," I answer.

"Look," Jane says, her eyes glued to the road in front of us. "Derek had a strep infection when he was a little kid. Almost everyone gets strep at one time or another, but his got so bad it damaged his heart permanently. I just thought you should know that in case you were thinking this was your fault or something."

I flash back to what Derek told me about his college days as we sat in that coffeehouse: "Bad luck," he said. "Health stuff." Well, *that* was an understatement.

"Derek had just been through heart surgery to fix a valve when I met him," Jane is saying. "It hadn't gone well, and he'd almost died. But he didn't die, and then we met, and I fell totally, head over heels in love." She sighs. "God, I really thought I was over being angry at you both."

"It's only been, like, a week." I'm not trying to be snotty with her (for once), but really, doesn't the whole grief thing usually take a while?

"You're right," she says. "And even though the sight of you makes me a little sick to my stomach, if I'm going to be completely honest . . ."

I'm not exactly thrilled to see you, either, I think.

". . . I still thought it was important for you to know that Derek knew he could—you know—go at any time. It's why he tended to . . . act a little wild sometimes. And why I always seemed to let him get away with it, I guess. Does that make any sense?"

She pauses, and I force myself to breathe. Even though my brain is having a hard time processing what she just said, I already feel weight being lifted from my shoulders, like my conscience has been paroled: I'm not responsible for killing somebody after all—not completely, anyway. *You're saying I didn't do your husband to death?* I almost want to ask her, but it doesn't seem entirely appropriate, given the circumstances. So instead, I just let out my own deep breath and say, "Yeah, it makes sense. I mean, if I had heart trouble I'd probably do crazy stuff, too."

"Not that what you did was okay," Plain Jane says, cutting me off. "Not by a long shot."

We ride the rest of the way in silence, and ten minutes later I'm standing in the entry hall of the house Derek once shared with his wife. It's not fancy, but it's not a dump, either: *The walls could use a new coat of paint,* is the first thing I think, *something other than beige.* Knowing Derek lived here is already more than I wanted to know about him.

Plain Jane looks like she doesn't know what to do with her hands; she puts them in the pockets of her cardigan and then takes them out. "Well, I guess I should give you the tour," she says finally.

I follow her into the living room, and an old man is sitting in a recliner there, his eyes glued to a TV screen where Chuck Norris in a black cowboy hat and badge is getting ready to serve some guy a knuckle sandwich.

"This is my father, Earl," Jane tells me. Then, in a louder voice, she says, "Dad? This is Brianna. She's going to be staying with us for a while."

We'll see about that, I think.

Earl beams up at me from the chair and starts positioning his arms and feet to stand. It looks like it's going to be a major production.

"You don't have to get up," I tell him.

Settling back into the chair and still beaming, he holds out his hand for me to shake. "A guest," he says. "How perfectly splendid." There's a little pile of crinkly candy wrappers on the table next to him, and he reaches into his shirt pocket for a new, wrapped piece, which he holds out to me. "Werther's Original?"

"No, thanks."

"Nuh-uh," Jane scolds him, scooping up the wrappers and gently taking the piece from his hand. "You know what Dr. Mueller said about your sugar intake. Give me the ones in your pocket, too."

Earl pouts but does what he's told. Then he turns his attention back to the TV, where a thorough ass-kicking is now in progress. "Give 'em hell, Walker," he says, chuckling.

As Jane leads me out of the room she whispers, "He has Alzheimer's. Derek and I, we've been—*I've* been taking care of him for about a year now. He's a sweetheart, but it's not easy."

"What about your mom?" I ask her.

"She passed away during my first year of college. Cancer."

"Oh, wow, I'm sorry," I say. "It must have been hard." And I immediately want to smack myself upside the head, because could I have said something more obvious?

Jane either doesn't hear my comment or she ignores it, focusing instead on giving me a tour not unlike the one Mo gave me a week earlier when I showed up at Hope House: she shows me where my room is and then points out the bathroom, which she tells me I'll have to share with Earl. "You'd probably like to take a shower, I guess."

"Why? Do I look dirty to you?" It comes out harsher than I mean for it to, and Plain Jane looks down.

"That's not what I—" she starts to say, but I hold up a hand.

"Sorry. I'm just really tired."

"Well," she says, rubbing her palms against the sides of her jeans. "That is certainly understandable. Just, you know, let me know if you need anything."

"Okay." Then, as she turns toward the door, I say, "Mrs. Playne?

"Please," she says. "You're a guest in my house while you're here, not a student. Call me Jane."

"Okay. Um, Jane?"

"Yes?"

"I—I just want to say . . ." But where do I even start? There's so much I could say, everything from *I'm sorry for being such a jerk to you this year* to *I didn't know he was your husband.* But how do you just come out and say something like that? "I just want to say . . . good night."

The bed has been made up, right down to one of those fake pillow cases you have to set aside before going to sleep because you know you're not supposed to put your head on it. And even though I know the bed has probably been fancy like that—fancy to let special guests know how welcome they are—even before Derek spent part of his last night in my very unfancy bed at Keisha's house, it still weirds me out. So I sleep on the floor that first night, just curl up there, curl into myself, because it's a skill I have, being able to sleep anywhere at any time.

I wake up in the middle of the night having to pee so bad it hurts. I'm disoriented at first, and I look around the dark room, trying to figure out where I am. Am I at Hope House? Keisha's house? Jolene's? Then I remember. A clock on the bedside table above my head says 4:04, and I reach up to switch on the bedside lamp so I can find the door and tiptoe to the bathroom. Passing Plain Jane's room on my way back, I notice that her door is open partway and her light is on. I don't see her, but I do see a shadow moving back and forth across the light coming through the door. I hear her voice, too. It's a little louder than a whisper, and it almost sounds like she's chanting.

"What am I doing? What am I doing? What am I doing?" her voice says, and after listening to it for a while, I tiptoe back to the guest room and close the door behind me as quietly as possible before curling back up on the floor and trying to get a little more sleep.

Finally, right about the time the sky starts getting lighter, I hear something in the kitchen, Plain Jane getting the morning started in her bathrobe, probably. Fixing breakfast like normal people do, even though it's clear she's about the furthest thing from normal there is—further than me, even. And that's saying something.

I reach for my backpack and unzip the main compartment.

Miraculously, there's a clean pair of underwear bunched up in there. My jeans and T-shirt aren't quite as clean, but they'll have to do, because I've already decided that today's the day I start working at being normal again. I don't care how awkward it is waking up in Derek's house and making small talk with his widow over tea and crumpets (or whatever it is English teachers eat in the morning).

I am a Lowell High flyer, and today is the day I go back to high school and reclaim my life.

11

signed, desperate

JANE OFFERS ME a ride to school on my morning back, and my instinct is to refuse it. There's no bus stop near her house, though, and when I look at the clock and calculate how long it would take for me to walk, I realize I'd get there halfway through first period. I definitely don't want to draw that kind of attention to myself, so I accept the ride, figuring we'll get to school early enough to avoid being seen by too many people.

I figure wrong: as my bad luck would have it, a couple of the swim team jocks see me getting out of her car as they come out of the locker room after morning practice. Their eyebrows go up when I walk away from the car fast (but not fast enough to keep Jane from calling out, "I'll see you at home—I mean, in class—later"), and I know for a fact they won't have anything better to do today than blow this totally out of proportion.

The fallout starts during homeroom as Mr. Gupta's calling roll. When he gets to my name a bunch of guys in the back of the classroom (including one of the swim team jocks who saw me getting out of Jane's car) start coughing. At first it sounds like a random thing, like they all inhaled something into their lungs at once.

"Brianna Taylor," Gupta says again, but the coughing only gets louder.

"Bru-*hown*-noser," one of the guys coughs into his fist. A few students laugh, including Jules, who hasn't looked me in the eye since I walked in.

Gupta glances up from his grade book and says, "That's enough of that." And for a few seconds, it seems like there will be nothing more.

Then: "*Cough*—Playne'sbitch—*cough*," somebody else blurts into the silence. This time, everybody laughs—everybody except me and Mr. Gupta, that is. I stare straight ahead at the wall like I'm the only one in the room. Mr. Gupta stares straight up at the heavens, like his next directions for dealing with a class full of teenage ass clowns might come down from there. And it's pretty clear by this point that everybody in the class—maybe everyone in the school—knows what happened.

During English, nobody says a word, which is almost worse than the obnoxious comments in homeroom. Plus, Jane should get an Oscar for how well she acts like nothing out of the ordinary has happened. When she's going through all the homework and sees that mine is missing, she says the same thing she always says when a student flakes out: "Brianna, can I expect to see your homework turned in by tomorrow?"

I know she's probably doing it to show everyone that life in her classroom will proceed as usual and that there will be no favoritism, but for some reason it bugs the hell out of me.

"Whatever," I say, rolling my eyes like I used to do—showing everybody how over the whole thing I am.

I sneak a glance around the classroom to see if my eye roll communicated all I meant it to, but all I see is a bunch of mutes who refuse to so much as glance at me or Jane. Paul Schmitty looks like he might gnaw his pencil in half from anxiety, Alison Goldman is biting her lower lip, and absolutely nobody is laughing.

Plus, the fact that Jane doesn't fight back, that she continues to carry on like nothing has happened, bugs me even more than her comment about my missing homework.

After that, I am avoided for the rest of the day—at lunch, in the hallways between classes, and even by Kimmy and Charlotte, which is the part that hurts the most.

But the icing on the cake of my day happens that afternoon during cheer, when Jules decides to study a chip in her nail polish rather than spot me like she's supposed to. When I come out of a not-so-graceful basket toss and start to slip through the arms of one of the base girls whose job it is to catch me, there's nobody there to back her up. I keep falling until the back of my head hits the floor, and the sound it makes is not unlike the sound Derek's head made when it hit the bedside table at Keisha's house. For several seconds I don't feel any pain at all, just a numb kind of floatiness.

Jules's response to the whole thing is to get completely defensive. "What?" she says while I'm sitting on the sidelines holding ice cubes wrapped in a T-shirt to the back of my head and Coach Kristy is asking her what happened. "She just slipped."

When Coach comes over and asks me how I'm doing, I say, "Fine. I'm fine." But the truth is it hurts. A lot. Also, I can already feel a big goose egg forming just above the base of my skull. "I'm going to head back home in a minute," I tell Coach. Doubt flashes across her eyes for a second, and then she glances back at the other girls on the squad, who are waiting for her orders to start practice back up or not. "Really, Coach," I assure her. "I'm fine."

Jane told me this morning that she'd be in meetings for a few hours after school, which is probably just as well. After the stunt

I pulled in English, she's probably going to ask me to leave her house anyway. I can't say I'd blame her.

As I'm walking back to her house after practice, I start to not feel so good. I start to feel so bad, in fact, that I have to stop and hold on to a telephone pole. And then I throw up my cafeteria lunch in some bushes next to the sidewalk. It is totally embarrassing, but I feel so horrible by that point that I don't care, even when a car horn honks and some jerk yells "Yeah!" out the window as he drives by. All I know is the fall messed me up, and I just hope I don't end up with brain damage or worse.

There's a free walk-in clinic a couple of blocks away from the school. I know this because I once went there with Jules when she had an appointment to get tested for STDs. They gave her a brown lunch bag full of condoms when the appointment was over, and when Jules and I got back to her house we sat on her bed going through them. There were flavored condoms, colored condoms, condoms in little cases made to look like gold coins. "Imagine getting these in your Christmas stocking instead of chocolate coins," Jules said, and we laughed until our stomachs hurt.

I'm not laughing now, though, and somehow I make it to the clinic without puking any more. A sticker on the door reads THIS IS A SAFE HAVEN FOR NEWBORNS, and I have a momentary, crazy thought that maybe I could pin a note on myself before walking in: *Please take care of this teenager because she's kind of like a big baby. Signed, Desperate.*

I remember how there was something strangely comforting about the ER the night Derek died—the plastic-covered chairs, Conan on the TV. Maybe this place will be the same, I think, and the thought makes me smile. It must be a crazy smile, though, and I must not look so hot in general, because the lady at the check-in desk gets all wide-eyed when I walk through the door.

"Are you alone?" she asks me.

"Yes."

"Are you ill?"

I nod.

"I can tell," she says, handing me a clipboard. "You look terrible. No offense. We'll get you back there as quick as we can, but first I'll need you to fill out some forms."

"Okay."

"Can I call someone for you? A parent, perhaps?"

"Don't bother," I tell her, not looking up from the clipboard. I can feel her eyes on me the whole time I'm filling out the new-patient information form. As soon as I'm done and she's gotten the information she needs from my insurance card (at least I still have medical going for me, since Jolene qualifies for all the state handouts and I haven't filled out the emancipated minor forms yet), a nurse comes into the waiting area and tells me to follow her. She takes my temperature outside the bathroom, then hands me a Dixie cup and a marker.

"I'll need a urine sample," she says,

"Why? It's my head that hurts."

"It's just standard, hon."

"Fine." I head into the bathroom, and after writing my name on the cup and filling it with the 'sample,' I look in the mirror. The lady up front was right: I look like roadkill. My skin's pale, my hair's a mess, and it looks like I haven't slept in a week. Which, when I stop to think about it, isn't really an exaggeration. Plus, it's beyond humiliating to hand a cup of your own pee to a complete stranger. I do it anyway, though, because I'm in no shape to argue.

The nurse shows me to an exam room. "Are you sexually active?" she asks, handing me a paper gown.

I shake my head, and she jots something down on her clipboard before leaving the room so I can change.

When she comes back twenty minutes later her face is softer

somehow. A doctor comes in with her. He's middle-aged, with hair that's just starting to turn gray at his temples, and his eyes look tired but not unkind.

"Ms. Taylor," he says. "I'm Dr. Marquez. I'll be checking your pupils and your reflexes in general, because it sounds like you had a nasty fall. Potential concussion issues aside, however, I do have another question for you."

"What's that?" I'm sighing at this point, because I already just want the poking and prodding and testing to be over.

Dr. Marquez doesn't seem to notice my impatience, because he's sighing, too, as he looks into my eyes and asks, "Are you aware that you're pregnant?"

12

Brianna on the brink

JANE'S NOT HOME when I get back from the clinic, which is a good thing because this way maybe I can get my bearings a little. Earl is home, though, and I just stand there in the kitchen for a minute listening to the sound of the TV and wishing there was someone I could tell about the exciting new show that's apparently airing right this very moment in my womb.

"Is that a girl or a robber?" Earl calls from the next room.

"Just me," I call back.

"Well, come say hello, Me."

I set down my backpack and the now-squishy ice pack Dr. Marquez gave me after announcing that I was not, in fact, concussed, which is the only piece of good news I've had in a week. Then I go to the TV room, where Earl grins at me from his recliner.

"That Mary Tyler Moore," he says. "What a gal."

"Yeah?" I say, taking a seat on the couch. I watch an old black-and-white rerun with him for a while.

"So, what's up, Sunshine?" Earl clicks off the TV, and it occurs to me that he seems pretty clear-headed.

"I don't know," I tell him. "Nothing much, I guess."

"Hm. Why don't I believe you?"

"I don't know," I say again, looking down at my suddenly fidgety hands.

Earl is quiet for a moment. Then he says, "Well, I certainly don't want to be a buttinsky," and begins preparations for getting up from the recliner. "I'll leave you to your thoughts."

Before I can stop myself, I blurt out, "Wait. There is something." And it's only when I start telling Earl about my doctor's appointment and the stuff leading up to it that I finally begin to feel emptied of some of the guilt and shame I've been feeling since the night Derek died.

It's clear from Earl's furrowed brow and the way he whispers "Oh, no" that he's shocked by what he's hearing, even though I leave out Derek's name and a bunch of other details (mainly because I have a feeling Jane's never told him exactly why I moved in). Still, he manages to be the perfect listener. If he's judging me, he hides it well by nodding and making sympathetic sounds at all the right places in my story, and when I'm finished, he just looks at me in concerned silence. Finally, he leans forward in his chair and holds out both of his hands. They're a little like tree bark, with prominent knuckles and veins. I lean forward, too, and put my hands in his.

"Now, listen to me," Earl says. "You're a good girl. And you're strong, too. I can see it. You're a lot like my Janey that way."

"Okay," I say in a barely-there voice as something shifts a little in my chest.

"We're going to get through this," Earl says. "Do you hear me?"

It's all I can do to nod.

"The three of us together. Like Musketeers. We're going to get through this."

Which is, of course, all it takes for me to finally be able to cry.

Earl stays where he is, patting my hand and passing the box of tissues, and it occurs to me that this simple, important thing—sitting and talking with a kind, older person who cares—is something I've never experienced.

"Please don't tell Jane," I say when the tears finally stop.

Earl responds by reaching into his shirt pocket and winking as he holds out a piece of candy wrapped in crinkly paper.

About an hour later, when Earl has retired to his room and Jane's still not home, I do something for no sane reason that I can begin to come up with: I head down the hall and push open the door of the bedroom she shared with Derek.

One of the walk-in-closet doors is open, and I step in toward the hanging clothes. Then I reach up and pull a little metal chain attached to a light fixture so I can see.

If Jane has started getting rid of Derek's stuff, she hasn't yet gotten to this closet, because half of it is taken up by men's shirts, khakis, and blazers. I open the other closet door to expose Derek's things, and then I brush my fingertips over all of it, just like I did with the things at Jules's house.

I pull one of Derek's white oxford shirts from its hanger, and as I bring it to my face it occurs to me that I have no idea what he did for a living. I'm standing there in a sort of daze, inhaling traces of his musky scent with my face buried in that shirt, when a voice behind me says, "How long were you seeing him?"

I drop the shirt as if it has suddenly burst into flames.

"I was just—" I say, spinning around to face Jane, who's standing there in the doorway of her bedroom with a glass of wine in her hand. Which means she's been home long enough to set down her things, pour the wine, and come down the hall—and I was completely oblivious to all of it.

"He was wearing that shirt the night we met," she says, her

eyes narrowed in a way that makes me think my behavior in class earlier today must have pissed her off more than I thought. "It was a blind date. By the end of the night he'd swept me off my feet and told me I was a diamond in the rough that he wanted to make shine. That I was the kind of loyal, trustworthy girl he'd been searching for his whole life. Which was a little impulsive, don't you think?"

"I guess." What the hell else am I supposed to say?

"So, how long were you seeing him?" she asks again, raising the wineglass to her mouth and taking a gulp, her eyes never leaving my face. I wonder how often she drinks, because it clearly doesn't come naturally to her. Her speech is already starting to get a little slurred.

"Okay," I say, gesturing in a lame way at the closet and at Derek's clothes. "First of all, I'm—I'm sorry about, um, this." I pick the oxford up off the floor and put it back on its hanger as fast as I can, reminding myself not to let my newest secret slip out; clearly, Jane is close enough to the edge already. "Second of all," I continue, "it was one night. That's all. And I swear I didn't know who he was. I had no idea he was married, or I would have—"

"You would have what?"

"I would have *never* done . . . what we did," I say.

I can't tell if she believes me or not. Not that it probably matters either way, because this whole thing is starting to feel more bogus by the minute, and she should just go ahead and tell me to leave if that's where this is heading. True, I'll have nowhere left to go if she kicks me to the curb, but it seems like it wouldn't matter at this point. "Just so you know," I tell her. "Derek knew it was a mistake."

"How do you know that?"

And suddenly I'm completely wiped out from the entire day, not to mention the tension between me and Jane and the general weirdness of having this conversation while I'm standing in Derek's closet. "Because he wondered out loud what the hell he was doing with me," I answer.

"He did?" Jane is frowning, like she's not sure she can trust me to tell her the truth.

"Yeah," I say. "He did. I should have known something was wrong when he said that, but I didn't really have a chance to ask questions. And then he . . . well, you know, he fell down." As I think of how ungraceful Derek's fall was and think of the sound his head made as it hit the table, the back of my own head starts to throb. I put my hand there to feel the goose egg and wince.

"What happened to you?"

"Long story," I tell her. "I hit my head."

"You should ice that."

"The doctor gave me a pack. It melted."

"Ah, doctors," Jane says, apparently lost in boozy thought. She pauses before continuing. "I guess I need to start sending back Derek's disability checks. Remind me to do that, will you?"

When I just stare at her, my face a blank, she says, "Heart condition? He had no job? Hello?" Then she lifts a hand likes she's going to do the *Anybody home?* knock on my forehead, but I duck out of the way.

And even though I can tell she's a little too out of it to give me a clear answer, I go ahead and ask the question that's been bugging me the most. "Why did you bring me here, Jane? Why did you take me in?"

She pauses again with her glass in midair. Then she knocks back the last of the wine, wipes her mouth with the back of her hand, and lets out a belch. "Hell if I know," she says before turning around and leaving the room, leaving me to stand in the closet surrounded by a dead man's clothes.

I'm still there, trying to get a grip on what just happened, when Jane returns, unsteadily, to the bedroom with a bag of frozen peas and plops them into my hand. "Maybe I'm just a wee little bit lost," she says. "Like you. Maybe that's why I took you in." That last part comes out all muzzy, like *Maybe thashwhy tookyin,* and then she says, " 'Night, roomie," and wobbles over to the bed, where she plants herself facedown on top of the covers, arms and legs splayed out like the limbs of a starfish. She's already snoring when I click off the closet light and tiptoe into the hallway.

I keep the peas pressed to the goose egg as I lie there in "my" room on what has been, without question, the most surreal day of my entire life—and not just because it's my first day as an officially pregnant teenager. I've decided to sleep on the bed instead of the floor this time—fancy pillow sham be damned—and the headboard creaks every time I move. I wonder if Jane meant what she said about being lost like I am, and I wonder how long it will take her to kick me out when she finds out I'm pregnant. Because if one thing is certain, it's that I will always get kicked out. It's just a matter of time. The predictability of that fact is almost soothing, and the thing that finally helps me drift off to sleep is thinking of the word "good-bye" in as many different languages as I can: *sayonara, arrivederci, adieu, adios. . . .*

When I head to the kitchen for cornflakes the next morning, Jane is sitting at the table rubbing her temples. I can hear low applause coming from the TV in the living room, which means Earl is settled into his recliner for the morning. I know I probably won't be able to keep the cereal down, since even the thought of food makes my stomach do queasy little flip-flops, but I get a bowl from the cupboard anyway. From the half-eaten toast and still-full cup of coffee on the table in front of her, it looks like Jane is struggling to keep things down this morning, too.

"I've been sitting here thinking about how utterly embarrassed I am about last night," she says without looking at me. "I don't usually do things like that, like getting drunk."

"It's okay." I say it mainly so she'll drop the subject and I can get on with the day.

"It's just . . . ," she continues, as if I've asked for some kind of explanation. "I'm working through all these things right now. Derek dying, my dad's dementia. And then I walked into my room after a really hard day yesterday, and there you were holding that shirt, and I guess it all just came to a head."

"Seriously. It's okay."

Jane ignores me, though. "Truth?" She asks this like I'm supposed to answer her, but then she doesn't wait for my answer. "Sometimes I think Derek never would have looked at me twice if I wasn't so good at taking care of people. Because Derek needed someone to take care of him. He needed it, but he also hated needing it. And I was, you know, in *love,* so of course I was willing to do whatever I could. But he needed excitement, too, and I wasn't very good at providing that. He needed to live on the edge so it didn't always feel like his funky heart was in control."

"Not that it's an excuse for what happened," I add. I'm trying to keep up with her by this point, to go with the flow as I pour my cereal, but I can't help letting my mind wander back to the night I met Derek at the Frog, how it was his confidence, his lack of fear, that finally won me over. And yes, the sense of anything-can-happen that seemed to follow him around was pretty exciting, too.

"No," Jane says. "Not that it's an excuse."

And that's when I set the box of cornflakes on the counter, take a deep breath, and turn to face her full-on. "Maybe it would be better if I *wasn't* here," I say. "You know, so you could work through your stuff."

Jane stops rubbing the sides of her head and looks at me with her bloodshot eyes. "Don't be ridiculous, Brianna," she says. "You have nowhere else to go, and I'm not about to send you back to that shelter. Plus, it's a good way to get back at the stupid cow who cornered me in the faculty lounge last week."

Whoa. "What stupid cow?"

"It's . . . I don't even know if I should be telling you this," she says, looking wincey and uncertain all of a sudden.

I just stare.

"Okay," she says, sighing. "It was last week after the memorial. One of the teachers—who shall remain nameless, by the way—cornered me in the teachers' lounge and said, 'You must feel vindicated right about now with that Brianna Taylor hiding away in shame. Even her mother and sister don't have a clue where she is—not like they seemed to care when we called them.' "

And all of a sudden I'm shrinking inside a little, thinking, *A teacher at school said that about me?* I mean, I know most of the teachers at Lowell aren't my biggest fans. Still, it's like a punch to the gut to know that at least one of them is actually happy to hear I'm suffering.

"And, you know," Jane continues, "I had to think about it for a second. Because I did feel sort of like Derek's death was being avenged, like you were having to pay your dues. I mean, here's this . . . this *girl* who slept with my husband, right?"

I flinch, but I don't say anything.

"But then I remembered that you were just that. A girl. And I won't be the kind of person who takes pleasure in seeing a kid suffer. I refuse to be that person, Brianna. Do you understand?"

"Maybe."

"I guess what I'm trying to say is, it would be really easy for me to see you as some sort of home-wrecker Lolita and hate you for it. But I can't deal with hating you on top of everything else."

"I've dealt with worse," I tell her, so tired again all of a sudden.

She looks at me without saying anything, and at first I can't tell what kind of look is in her eyes. When I realize it's pity, my gut twists.

"Who's Lolita?" I ask her.

"She's a character in a book by Vladimir Nabokov. Maybe you'll read it someday. Anyway," she says, standing up from her chair and yanking the belt of her robe a little tighter around her waist like *Okay, I'm ready to take on this day.* "You wanted to know last night why I took you in. It's because I refuse to hate you."

As usual, I'm not sure quite how to take this, but I do know there's no time for another headshrinking session right now. Jane and I have to get dressed and get going pronto, because I'm sticking by my decision to keep showing up at school no matter what else happens. This is mainly because I won't be allowed to cheer if I don't, and I am still determined to hold on to *that* last little shred of normal, even if everything else in my life is becoming more psychedelic by the moment.

It's that determination that carries me through the next few weeks, and it's a huge relief when the nasty digs about me and Jane let up a little, replaced by nasty digs about other people's drama. Things aren't perfect at school, but they're getting closer to bearable, and I hang in there with cheer, even though practice has been a pretty exhausting experience ever since I hit my head. I don't know if it's because of the pregnancy or because I feel like I'm not really a part of the squad anymore. I mean, I'm technically part of it, but nobody really talks to me. Even Charlotte and Kimmy avoid eye contact.

It isn't long before my squad woes take a backseat to bigger problems, though, because in no time flat I find myself having to work double-time at keeping my "delicate condition" a secret.

In the month after my visit to the clinic and Jane's night of wino confession, it actually scares me how fast my boobs grow while the rest of me basically stays the same size. Normally, I'd love to move up a bra size, but this is ridiculous. My chest actually hurts. Also, my stomach is starting to get a little flubbery, which means I'm not able to button my skinny jeans all the way up anymore.

Since it's the end of October anyway, and since being at school lately feels more and more like I'm alone in a creepy Halloween forest at night with all sorts of creatures hiding in the trees waiting to attack, I do what I have to do to stay incognito: I start dressing in the baggiest sweats I can find. Because, let's face it: it's better for people to see me dressing like a slob than to figure out what it is I'm hiding. Plus, here's another lovely detail: during the first month after finding out about the baby—which I have started thinking of as the Bun in the Oven (the Bun for short)—I have to throw up on a fairly regular basis. This means I just walk out of whatever classroom I happen to be in at the time and head for the nearest bathroom as fast as I can. Since most of my female teachers don't seem to know what to do or say when I'm around anyway (probably because they're worried about their husbands and sons becoming my next victims), they usually just ignore it.

It goes without saying that I no longer sit on the hallway railing Jules and I used to share. Our lockers are still practically adjoining, but we don't bother to look at each other—much less talk—anytime we happen to be there at the same time. And where the two of us used to own the classes we took together, now it's just Jules, which is probably how she always wanted it anyway.

It isn't too long before I start to feel so lousy that I have to stop going to cheer practice altogether—which, of course, means I'm off the squad. It's just as well, I guess, since I can't get the skirt zipped up all the way anymore. Coach Kristy is pretty nice about it when she gives me the bad news, but I can tell she's disappointed.

"Are you okay, Bree? Do you need to talk about... you know... stuff?"

I can't help worrying that maybe Coach is just interested in gossip like everyone else, so I shake my head and tell her I'm sorry for flaking out.

After that, it's a long downhill slide into grody oblivion. Since I'm already living in sweats 24/7, it seems pointless to keep wearing makeup and worrying so much about my hair, which does just fine barely brushed and pulled back with a rubber band—and to think I used to harsh on Jane for being unnecessarily fugly. I also start zoning out in all my classes, because what's the point? It's not like I have to maintain a B average to stay on the squad anymore. When I start practically sleeping through English, though, Jane takes notice.

"You okay?" she asks, glancing at me in the car on the way home from school one day.

"Yeah, I'm fine. Just tired."

But the truth is, no matter how much I try to hold on to my last shred of normal, it's being unraveled by fear—fear of being found out, fear of not knowing what to do, fear of becoming a mother. Of becoming *my* mother, who got pregnant with Keisha when she was just about the age I am now. Really, it's just too much to think about, which is why I try—unsuccessfully—not to.

In second-period technology, I use the computer to doodle rather than diagram, which is what we're supposed to be doing. With the paintbrush tool I draw a picture of a stick-figure girl with a big belly who's standing on the edge of a cliff. A grizzly bear is standing on its hind legs right behind her, and the girl's eyes are wide as she looks down at the canyon below. I even draw little drops of sweat popping out from her head. *That's me,* I think when the picture's done. *Brianna on the brink.*

13

graffiti

ONE MORNING in mid-November when I'm getting ready for school, I can't get my sweatshirt to stay pulled down over my rapidly growing bump, and I realize for the first time that sweats are just not going to cut it anymore. I've been staying in my own private La-La Land as long as humanly possible, but it looks like La-La Land is over now. I'm almost three months pregnant, and I don't know if it's because I have a small frame or what, but I officially no longer own a single piece of clothing that fits.

"Damn it," I say into thin air as I sit down on the bed in a kind of daze. Then, after a few minutes, I get up, find a skirt with the stretchiest waistband possible, notch the elastic with a pair of scissors to make it stretch even farther, and then pair it with the oversized man's T-shirt I usually use for a nightgown. It's getting close to Thanksgiving, so I've started bundling up the best I can, trying to look bulky all over instead of just in the boobs and belly. It's been so crazy warm out for November, though, that all the other girls are still going around in their painted-on jeans and miniskirts, which only makes me stick out more.

And apparently it's not bad enough that I have officially

become a serial fashion killer, because later that day, when I bend down to get something during chemistry, even the T-shirt pulls tight over my belly. Cindy Mason, my loudmouth lab partner, sees it and says, "Oh my God. What are you, pregnant or something?"

"Shut up," I say, giving her the Death Glare. "I'm just retaining water." But considering the way all the girls in the class are looking at each other all of a sudden, I know that excuse doesn't fly with them, not for a second.

Over the next few days, I catch people staring at my stomach and then giving these little secret looks to each other when they think I'm not paying attention. Then, one day at lunch, I'm standing in the cafeteria holding my tray and looking for a safe place to sit. This never happened pre-Derek, since Charlotte or some other cheerleader with a car would always drive a bunch of us off campus to grab frozen yogurt or a burger. There's no spot for me in anyone's car now, though, so I keep scanning the crowd until a voice behind me says, "Hey, Brianna. Why don't you come sit with us?"

I turn around and see Nathan Lumpke standing there. Nathan Lumpke—longtime worshipper of me and Jules. His hair is still slicked back, his skin still hasn't cleared up, and his shirt is unbuttoned even lower than usual. When I look where he's pointing I see a table overflowing with card-carrying members of the Brain Tribe. Several of them smile and wave at me in a hopeful sort of way; either I'm still valuable currency to some people at this school, or else they know a wounded antelope when they see one, and they're just offering me herd protection. Not too long ago I would sooner have let the lions feast on my entrails than be seen hanging with Nathan and his kind. But now? Now it's clear the easiest thing would either be to sit by myself at lunch or sit with the brains, who are as distracted by mathematical theorems and scientific hypotheses as I am by gestation.

I'm seriously considering his offer when a senior girl I've never met sidles up to me, smiling.

"Brianna, right?" she asks, and I nod.

"We were all just wondering," she says, and I'm either too slow or too hormonally disoriented to think what I should be thinking, which is *Uh-oh*. Instead, I just smile right back at her.

"Isn't there something that, you know, you might want to *share* with everybody?" The girl stares down at my stomach when she says this, and I look over at a table nearby, where a bunch of her senior friends sit, just watching the whole thing and waiting to crack up.

When the girl doesn't get a reaction from me, she walks away, shrugging at her friends and giggling. And more than anything at that moment, I wish Keisha still went to Lowell—the old Keisha, who, with rolled-up sleeves and a cigarette clenched between her teeth, would have kicked all their asses in the parking lot after school for harassing her little sister.

I long so badly for some kind of family connection at that moment, though, that I decide to call Jolene right after school. It's probably another stupid move, but does it really matter? Everyone at school is going to find out about the Bun sooner or later anyway. Plus, even if we've had our issues, a girl should tell her mother this kind of news before she tells anyone else, right?

"I know who you should go to for the abortion" is all Jolene says when I tell her how far along I am.

"I'm not getting an abortion."

"Oh, for crying— Why not?" Jolene demands.

Why didn't you abort me? I almost ask her. I don't, though (maybe because I'm afraid she'll say *I wish I had*). Because if there's one choice Jolene made that I can agree with, it's her decision to have me. Despite the number of times I've thought my life sucked, I've never wished—seriously wished—I'd never been born.

Like everyone else at school, I've heard the rumors about girls who had abortions, girls who supposedly ended their pregnancies for all sorts of reasons. Either they wanted to, or their boyfriends threatened to break up with them if they didn't, or their parents kicked them out and wouldn't let them come home until they made the problem go away. Thinking about those rumors now and listening to Jolene on the other end of the phone line makes me think that maybe I'm lucky, for once, not to have a boyfriend or involved parents. Because the decision to have or not have this baby is mine and mine alone.

"How's Larry?" I ask, changing the subject.

"Larry's business isn't really working out," Jolene says.

Big shock, I think. And when it's clear there's nothing more to say and I'm a major idiot (yet again) for thinking my mother would be supportive of my pregnancy or anything else in my life, I let the conversation die a natural death.

Of course, Jane has to pick that day to come home and say, "The holidays are coming up, and I've been thinking."

"Uh-oh," Earl says from his spot at the kitchen table, but Jane ignores him.

"We should have your mother over, Bree."

"That isn't necessary," I tell her.

"I know it's not necessary, but surely she wonders how you're doing. Have you been calling her? Keeping in touch?"

"I don't think you understand."

"Well, I'm not a mother, but I think she deserves to—"

It's Earl, of all people, who finally stops the madness. Sitting up a little in his chair in what is obviously one of his more lucid moments, he clears his throat and says, "Janey, listen. It sounds like Brianna's mother is just not that into her."

Jane and I both stop and stare at him.

"That's the best way anyone's ever explained it," I tell him.

Maybe it's because I'm still not over all the whispered classroom comments about me living with Jane. Or maybe it's because I can't stand the thought of being that much farther down on the social ladder when people find out I'm not just living with my English teacher but I'm pregnant with her dead husband's baby, too. Whatever it is, rather than just admitting to my condition at school, I work harder than ever to keep it hidden—even though that particular cat is clearly out of the bag, clawing the furniture and coughing up hairballs all over the place.

The day I finally have to face facts, I'm zoning out in fourth-period history when Mr. Mohler asks me to get the ancient world globe down from its shelf so he can show us all where Yugoslavia used to be. "Of course," Mohler says, glaring around at everybody, "you should all be sufficiently caught up on global events to know such a thing anyway."

And without thinking—for once without thinking, because just that day the nausea has decided to give me the tiniest little break—I get up from my desk, walk over to the shelves, and reach up for the globe. And when I do, it's like everyone in the class gasps at once, momentarily sucking all the oxygen out of the room.

I wouldn't be surprised if Mohler gasps, too, because the ever-fashionable man's T-shirt I chose to wear this morning rides up over my belly and sits bunched up right on top of it so that my abdomen—the House of Bun—is displayed in all its glory, big and round as the world globe I'm holding. Okay, so maybe that's an exaggeration because I'm only a few months pregnant and not yet sporting the classic round pregnant belly. Still, it's clear there's something going on inside my once famously flat abdomen, which now resembles a mound of risen bread dough with a Nerf ball hidden inside.

Nobody says a word as I walk to the front of the room, hand Mohler the globe, return to my desk, sit down, and flip open my book like nothing happened. I consider making a crack about who can find the old Yugoslavia on my belly the fastest. And it's at that moment I realize just how over the whole high school thing I really am.

Finally, one of the idiot guys at the back of the room breaks the silence: "Man, what did you *eat?*"

Widespread hilarity ensues. Because it's just so, so funny.

"Dang, Taylor," another one says, riffing. "If you wanted someone to put a baby in there, all you had to do was ask. I woulda been more than happy to help you out," which makes all his moron friends slap him on the back and start hooting like gorillas.

I, of course, have to stand up and leave the room as fast as I can so I don't start screaming or crying right in front of everybody, thus sealing my reputation as a complete, knocked-up mental case. Mr. Mohler scribbles out a hall pass for me in about half a second, and I grab it from him as I head out the door.

Blinking back tears and trying to keep from hyperventilating, I get to the nearest girls' bathroom as fast as I can and lock myself in a stall to think about just how much my life sucks (and maybe to throw up, too, since the nausea is back in major waves all of a sudden in what feels like a vomit tsunami about to hit shore).

As I'm sitting there, a new piece of graffiti on the inside of the stall door catches my eye. Someone has drawn a Lowell High cheerleader, only this one is barefoot and missing a tooth, and she has braids sticking straight out from the sides of her head like Pippi Longstocking. Also, the top of the hillbilly cheerleader's uniform is pushed out by her big, bulging belly. There's an arrow pointing there with the words BABY ON BOARD printed next to it. And when I squint and look closer I can see the letters B for Brianna and T for Taylor on the front of the cheerleader's sweater along with a Power Ranger tattoo on her thigh—as if I need further proof that it's a picture of me.

My hall pass is a sweaty, crumpled ball of paper inside my fist, and I remember that first day of freshman year when I was still just a fashion-challenged kid held in awe by Goddess of Hotness Jules Hill, who told me in this very bathroom that I had great hair and that the guys were going to love me. I remember how it felt like I'd been blessed when she touched my head and walked out.

Now I throw the soggy hall pass on the floor and woof my cookies right into the toilet. Afterward, I splash cold water all over my face and march to the school office.

"What do I have to do to get out?" I say to the first person I see, who happens to be Ms. Grimes, the gray-haired and gray-sweatered secretary who has been at Lowell forever and who probably sleeps in some chamber behind the main office at night.

Grimes just looks at me over the rims of her old-lady bifocals and says, "Pardon?"

"To get out of here," I repeat slowly, like she's deaf or not quite fluent in English. "To. Drop. Out. What do I need to do?"

Grimes probably never even considered dropping out. She probably busted her butt all the way through high school and maybe even some college, but just look where she is now—sitting in a forty-year-old office with microscopic bits of asbestos and lead probably raining down on her every day.

"Oh, honey, you're not dropping out" is all she says to me now. Then she goes back to licking envelopes like she has just solved my life in about three seconds.

14

How Well Do You Know Your BFF?

EVEN THOUGH I haven't said anything to Jane about my conversation with Ms. Grimes, there must be something in the air, because I wake up late that night and Jane's kneeling by the side of my bed. At first I think, *Here we go again with the crazy,* but then I see in the faint glow of the night-light that she's not drunk, and she's not kneeling there in a creepy or scary way—not like that one boyfriend of Jolene's who liked to take pictures of me as I slept, and not like Keisha just before she kicked my ass out of her house.

"The toilet in the faculty lounge wasn't working today," Jane whispers, and even though my head is still filled with sleep fog, it occurs to me that this might be the most random thing anyone's ever woken me up to tell me.

"And you want me to fix it?" There's a right thing to say here. I just know it.

Jane is quiet for a minute. Then she says, "No, Brianna. What I'm trying to say is that all the teachers had to use that student bathroom near the office while our toilet was being fixed. And . . . I don't know if you know this, but . . ." She gets quiet again, like she doesn't know how to say what comes next. "But someone scribbled a pregnant girl with your initials. They're writing about you on the bathroom walls."

I just look at her, say nothing, and wish like hell I'd had the intelligence to scrub that stupid graffiti from the bathroom stall divider when I had the chance.

"You saw the pregnant cheerleader cartoon," I say finally, my head clearing a little.

"I saw the pregnant cheerleader cartoon."

"It was my initials that gave it away, huh?"

"Yes," Jane says. "That plus the braids and missing tooth." Then she completely cracks up. Her laugh is higher-pitched than usual, though, more like a chipmunk laugh, which freaks me out a little—until she starts to cry, which freaks me out even more. She cries silently, but her shoulders are shaking. And because she's gripping the edge of the bed as she kneels there, the bed starts shaking, too.

I don't know what to do, so I just lie there stiff as a board, so not ready for her tears on top of everything else.

For a long time Jane's sobbing is the only sound in the room—that and my heartbeat, which is booming in my ears as I try not to breathe at all. Then, out of nowhere, she takes a deep breath and blows it out, which makes me breathe again, too. "So, is it true?" she finally asks.

I don't even bother to lie. Instead, I just nod.

"Well. I suppose part of me suspected that. So you're what—three months now?"

"Three-plus," I say. "I'm due in May."

"How are you feeling?"

"I've been better. I'm getting pretty tired of all the throwing up and everything." I realize I'm speaking slowly, choosing my words carefully, because all of a sudden it feels like I'm driving on a narrow mountain road with lots of dangerous curves and a sheer cliff on one side. And the next thing Jane says doesn't help, because it's like an unexpected patch of black ice on that treacherous road.

"And you're sure it's Derek's? I mean, there hasn't been anybody—"

"Nobody," I say, cutting her off and sitting up in the bed.

"You know," Jane continues, "I never told you this, but a part of me thought I needed you here to help me make sense of this whole thing. So I could watch you and figure out the missing piece of the puzzle of why my husband cheated on me, and so I could make damn sure no one ever does that to me again. Now I realize . . . I don't know. It's like this baby changes everything. Almost like it's not about me and Derek anymore, and it's not about you and Derek, either. It's not about any of us anymore. Does that make sense?"

I nod again.

"And I don't know if that's a good or a bad thing," Jane goes on. "I don't know if I'm ready for me and Derek not to matter so much anymore."

"You guys still matter," I tell her, even though it sounds weird coming from me. "He just made a mistake, that's all."

"Yes," Jane says, "I suppose so." She swivels around with a sigh so she's leaning against the bed and not facing me anymore.

"I made a mistake, too," I say, glancing at the back of her head in the near-dark and so thoroughly depressed at this point that, really, I almost don't even care what I'm saying anymore. "I don't think I ever told you I was sorry. But I am sorry. And I promise you I didn't know he was married. Just in case you didn't believe me the first time."

Jane raises a hand and waves it in a don't-worry-about-it gesture, which would be totally appropriate if I had just, like, eaten her last potato chip or something. It seems too casual a response now, though, until it occurs to me that maybe the tables are turned: maybe it's Jane's turn to not have a clue how to respond.

"He didn't know I was underage, either," I say. I don't know why I'm spilling my guts to her like this now, but it's actually a little bit of a relief. And even though Jane's back has suddenly stiffened and I can tell she's so tense she isn't breathing, I keep going. Because I'm apparently getting a little high on telling the truth. "So please don't think he was, like, a child molester or anything. He seriously didn't know."

That's when Jane turns her face to me again. "How do you know this?" she asks, and her voice is like stone—hard and cold.

That's it, I think. *Now I've blown it for sure. Hello, street. Hello, homelessness. Hello, foster care.* "Because I lied to him," I tell her. "I told him I was twenty-one. I was with a bunch of friends that night, and we all lied. We were just playing, and we thought he was cute and funny, and then things got . . . got out of hand."

But Jane doesn't tell me to get out. She doesn't scream or cry or do anything dramatic. Instead, she drops her shoulders and says, "It's the little things I miss about him. He was funny. He made me laugh. And this might be a strange thing to say, but you probably miss him, too."

I have to think about that for a second. The truth is, I only knew Derek for a night. But he made me feel something—a confidence, a sense of being okay—that nobody else ever made me feel. *You're one of the lucky ones,* he said. And for the first time in my life I saw myself in a different light. Sitting in the dark with Jane, it occurs to me that I wish I could see him one more time, if only to tell him I'm sorry for lying, sorry for the part I played in making this mess. But do I miss him?

"A little," I say, looking at Jane. "Yeah."

"Can I ask you a personal question?" Jane says.

"Okay."

"Why did you wait so long to tell me about the baby?"

I don't know, I want to tell her. *Because I suck. Because I'm a coward. Because I haven't wanted to admit it even to myself.* What I do finally say is "I've already made your life a living hell, and this just seems to make it that much worse."

Unfortunately, I don't stop there.

"The very worst part of it is that I planned to torture you way back on the first day of school," I tell her. "Well, Jules planned it, but I went along. We were going to start after Christmas."

"What are you talking about?" Jane says, and I can hear the frown in her voice. "Why me?"

"Jules is just big into that kind of stuff. And . . . I don't know. It's like—"

"You're bullies."

I'm quiet for a minute, and then I say simply, "Yeah, we are. I mean, I *was.* When I was around Jules I was permanently starting to become a not-nice person. Not like I'm a total angel now or anything, and not like it was all Jules's fault. But it also had to do with, you know, your name."

"Yeah," she says, slumping back against the bed frame.

I don't say anything.

"Oh, come on, Brianna. It's not like it's hard to figure out. And don't think I didn't consider it when Derek asked me to marry him. I mean, Jane Playne? Please. But I loved him. And when you love someone, you don't care so much about things like that."

"I know there's no way to tell you how sorry I am—" I start to say, but Jane waves my words away again.

"You've already done that," she says. "I think we should move on."

"Okay."

"So have you thought about, you know... your options?"

"If you mean am I going to have an abortion, I'm not," I tell her, and sensing an interrogation, I feel my back stiffening like I saw hers do just a minute ago.

"Right," Jane says. "It's probably none of my business anyway."

"No," I tell her. "It's not that. I just didn't know how to bring it up before, and I guess I didn't want you to kick me out."

"What kind of a person would that make me?"

"I guess," I say. "Believe me, though. I've already thought it through, and I've also been lectured by Jolene. Besides, even if I wanted to end my pregnancy, I'm pretty far along. But I don't want to. And maybe that makes me delusional, or selfish. I don't know. I just... I guess I just feel like the Bun deserves a chance. Even if the world royally sucks sometimes."

"It does royally suck sometimes," Jane says. And then, like our agreement about world suckage settles everything, she's sitting up and blowing her nose in a way that lets me know she's getting that same can-do attitude I got when I first found out I was pregnant and was determined to stay on the squad. "So. What kind of prenatal care are you planning to get?"

"I—I don't know. I had that one visit at the clinic where the doctor told me I was, you know..."

"Did you make another appointment?"

"Not yet, but—"

"What sort of pain management are you considering for when the baby's born?"

"Jeez, Jane. Chill out, will you?"

"I'll try," she says, blowing one last time into her tissue. "I really will."

"You should," I tell her. I rest one hand on my stomach and

look out the window at the sky, which is turning the color of bleached denim. "Because this baby still has a ways to go, and I'm going to need you to pace yourself."

As far as I'm concerned, winter break can't come fast enough. It starts snowing the day after school gets out, but it's not like I'm going to strap on a snowboard or a pair of ice skates anytime soon. Instead, I spend most of my time reading whatever book Jane happens to have lying around, and when I'm not doing that, I'm cleaning the house or keeping an eye on Earl so Jane can run errands.

These things aren't part of the arrangement, but I got used to doing housekeeping when I lived with Keisha and Robby, and it's something I can do to help out until I get too huge. Plus, the truth is, I feel like I owe Jane something, especially considering the small detail of my pregnancy. Not that there's any way I can really make up for that.

On Christmas Eve I'm in the kitchen on my hands and knees, scrubbing the baseboards in one of Jane's baggy brown dresses (which fits me quite nicely now) because I've apparently decided it's my turn to look like one of Van Gogh's potato diggers. No doubt Jane would kill me for cleaning like this, but I seriously couldn't care less. I don't know if it's my pregnant-girl nesting instinct kicking in or what, but all of a sudden the house never seems clean enough. While I'm down there a man I've never seen before walks in and puts a bag of groceries on the table. It takes me a second to recognize him from one of the family photos in the hallway.

"You must be Brianna," he says, holding up a hand in greeting.

I start to hold one of my own sudsy hands out to him but then think better of it and wipe it on the back of the brown dress instead.

"I'm Janey's brother, Mark."

"Hi," I say, throwing the sponge into a bucket of soapy water. "Jane and Earl ran out to grab a pizza, but they should be back pretty soon. Are you coming to pick him up?"

Mark nods. "Yeah, it's about time I gave my sis a break," he says. "That old man's a helluva lot of work."

"Mmhm," I say.

"I love him, though. You know."

"Yeah," I tell him. "Me too." Because it's true. How can you not love someone who keeps a never-ending supply of Werther's Original candies on hand and whistles like one of the Seven Dwarfs when he falls asleep watching old reruns of *Walker, Texas Ranger*?

At that point all I want to do is finish up the floor, pour myself a cup of hot cocoa overflowing with marshmallows, and go back to my room to read, but Mark obviously wants to keep talking. "Janey got the lion's share of compassion in the family, that's for sure," he says. "Anyway, sorry to hear you got mixed up with ol' whatsisname."

It takes me a second to figure out he's talking about Derek, and because I totally can't believe he said that, I just sit there on my heels like an idiot.

"So the guy's health isn't so great, and he can't work, and blah, blah, blah. Still no excuse to break my sister's heart and destroy your life—"

"I had a little something to do with it, too," I correct him.

"Yeah, yeah," Mark says. "Like they say, it takes two, but the whole situation just stinks."

Jane picks that moment to walk through the door, with Earl shuffling along behind her. She's carrying two big, flat pizza boxes, and pepperoni fragrance wafts through the air of the kitchen in heavenly ribbons, activating my drool mechanism. She walks over to her brother and tilts her head sideways so he can kiss her cheek. Then, to me, she says, "What are you doing on the floor?"

"Henry!" Earl says, saving me from having to explain my nesting instinct. He beams at Mark and opens his arms wide for a hug.

"Dad. I'm Mark."

Jane and I sneak a look at each other, but Mark just rolls his eyes and laughs a little. Taking the pizzas from Jane and setting them on the counter, he holds out a hand to help me stand up and then dumps the sudsy water out of the bucket as I wash my hands.

Jane and her brother catch up on family stuff while we eat, and once both pizzas have been polished off (mostly by me, obviously), Mark stands up from his chair and stretches. "Well, it's probably time for us to hit the road."

"Dad's suitcase is in the hall," Jane tells him. "Packed and ready to go." To Earl she says, "Don't forget your pills, okay? And *no* candy."

"Okeydokey, Artichokey," Earl answers, winking in my direction. Then, as he follows his son out the door, he turns and waves to me and Jane like a little kid waving bye-bye to his parents.

"Bye, Earl," I call after him. "I'll miss you." It's no lie. During the month leading up to winter break I agreed to stay home with him after school, not just when Jane ran errands but when she had to stay late for meetings, too. Without fail, those afternoons puttering around the house while Earl watched his shows were the high points of my week, which is no doubt why the house feels so lonely the next morning when it's just me and Jane opening presents. I got her a discounted collection of poems by Victorian women with some of the money I'd socked away from my week at Hope House, and she got me a maternity bathrobe and matching slippers.

"How are you feeling?" she asks later as we're vegging out on the couch listening to a *Nutcracker* CD.

I'm thumbing through an issue of a teen magazine looking at prom dresses, and I shrug. "I couldn't do a scorpion or a toe touch if my life depended on it," I tell her, patting the Bun.

"Well, you have more important things to think about, anyway. Like school."

I still haven't told her about my conversation with Ms. Grimes, how I was *this close* to dropping out just a couple of weeks ago.

Jane leans closer to get a better look at the magazine I'm reading. "Why do girls torture themselves looking at these Photoshopped models?"

"Prom is coming up," I say. "It's tradition."

"I guess I did that, too, at your age. . . ."

"Which wasn't that long ago," I remind her.

"But the girls these days. Is it me, or do they just look so . . . drugged out and cheap?"

"It's you."

"Oh, knock it off."

"Hey," I say, changing the subject. "Here's a quiz: 'How Well Do You Know Your BFF?' "

"Yeah, I remember those quizzes," Jane says.

"Okay, so let's say we're best friends. I mean, not that we *are* or anything, but just—"

"—for the sake of the quiz," Jane says, ignoring my sudden blush.

"Right. For the sake of the quiz. Okay, I'll start. It asks what my BFF's favorite ice cream is. I'm going to guess vanilla."

"You're good," Jane says. "It *is* vanilla."

Of course *it's vanilla,* I think, and Jane must notice how hard

I'm trying not to laugh right in her face, because she reaches for the magazine.

"Here, let me try," she says. "I'm going to guess that my BFF's favorite animal is . . . a swan."

"Wrong. Cats are my favorite. They can take care of themselves."

Jane raises her eyebrows. "Okay, I'm going to say my BFF wants to be a dance teacher when she grows up."

"A dance teacher?" I laugh. "Seriously?" Then the smile leaves my face. "I don't know. Who knows what I even *can* be now." It sounds pathetic and self-pitying, but every time I think about one new way the rest of my life has already been defined, it seems like the future isn't even worth thinking about.

"Hey," Jane says, putting down the quiz. "Don't talk like that. What would you be if money or circumstances weren't an issue?"

I don't know why she's bothering with this little game of Let's Pretend, but I don't have the energy to get all bitchy like I usually would. So I decide to humor her instead. "Maybe . . . I don't know, some kind of social worker?"

"Are you serious?"

"Why? Do you think that's stupid?"

"No. No, I think it's really great, actually."

"I just figured, you know, there are probably a lot of other girls out there like me who could use more people to help them out. You know, what's that word . . . to advocate for them."

Jane sits up. "You know, you can make a decent living at social work, too, but you have to have a degree."

That's when I know it's time to come back from La-La Land and change the subject, because suddenly this conversation has become more ridiculous than the BFF quiz. Me, in college? As if I have a snowball's chance in hell of *that* happening. "I just threw it out there," I say quickly. "It's kind of a stupid idea."

"It's not stupid at all, Bree. I think you could stand to take yourself and your future more seriously."

"Yeah," I tell her, grabbing the magazine off her lap. "Whatever. Okay, so I'm guessing your favorite guilty pleasure is . . . Seriously, I have no idea." The thought of Jane having any kind of guilty pleasure has never crossed my mind.

Jane leans back, clearly happy to change the subject from the Future of Brianna to something that will make me less hostile. "Okay, this is going to sound silly, but I read trash. I'll admit it," she says with a little evil grin on her face. "If I have a few extra bucks, the first thing I'm probably going to pick up is a trashy tabloid. All those scandals—all that celebrity cellulite! It's just . . . brain candy. It's total escape, you know?"

I'm still cranky, though, so all I say is "Ooh, walking on the wild side there, Jane. You better be careful, or the next thing you know you'll end up spending all your savings on tabloids, panhandling for your next fix."

"Oh, stuff it, Brianna."

I have to admit, I'm a little proud of her for throwing the sarcasm right back at me, even if she's sitting there looking a little shocked at what she just said.

You go, girl, I want to say this time, because that's the kind of thing she probably thinks is part of the hip, new vocabulary of our time. What a dork.

The day is quiet after that. Jane heads to her room for a nap, and I spend a few hours on the couch looking out the window at the thin veil of snow draped across the baby pine trees in the front yard. When Jane's *Nutcracker* CD is on its third replay and I've had at least that many cups of virgin eggnog, I head down the hall to use the bathroom. On my way back to the couch I get a glimpse of Jane through the half-open door of her room. She's sitting on the floor next to a pile of clothes, and there's a big cardboard box in front of her. I decide it's as good a time as ever for me to stop acting like such a cow.

"What are you doing?" The second I ask it, Jane looks up at me, and I realize the clothes on the floor are Derek's, that they're the same khakis and shirts she caught me fondling and sniffing after I first moved in.

"Where do I start?" she says, sighing. "For one thing, I've been thinking about how I'd feel if I came across Derek's things while going through the bins at a secondhand store. And just today, for the first time since he died, I think it would be okay."

"That's big," I say. "Right?"

"Yeah, it is." She stops and looks at the pile. "And it also means it's time for a closet makeover. I'm bringing all this stuff to the Pay-Per-Pound."

I stand there looking at her for a moment, just watching her pick up a shirt—a last little bit of her past life. She stares at the shirt for a second and then places it gently in the cardboard box.

"You know what I think?"

Jane looks at me with her head cocked to one side.

"I think it's time for more than just a closet makeover."

"I don't know what—" she starts to say, but I shush her and hold out a hand to help pull her up and away from the pile of Derek's clothes.

I lead her into the living room and command her—silently, with one stern, pointed finger, like I'm the teacher here—to sit on the couch. Then I head back to my room for the plastic baskets full of my makeup stuff. I don't know what colors are going to work best for her yet, so I just bring everything. The first thing I hand her is an elastic band.

"What's this?"

"Are you kidding? It's a headband. You need to pull all your hair away from your face so we can get started."

She does it, but then she keeps trying to pull little strands out from under the band to partially cover her face.

"Pull all of it back," I say, tucking the strands under the elastic.

Again she pulls them forward, almost like she's not aware of what she's doing.

"Jane," I say. "Seriously. You're killing me." I make her tuck the hair back in this time, but the tense look on her face as she's doing it makes me realize something: Jane's hair is some sort of protection for her, like her knitted scarves probably are, too; maybe she needs these shields against the world. It makes me wonder what I've used as my own shields over the years. Power Ranger tattoos, most likely. Fishnets and black eyeliner, too.

"Hold still." I tell her to close her eyes and raise her eyebrows so I can do shadow. Those eyebrows are terrible—patchy and thin—so I color them in a little, too, before moving on to her lips and cheekbones. When I'm done, she takes off the headband and shakes her hair out, looks at me.

I reach up and brush her bangs aside a little, tucking the longer strands behind her ears. "Wow," I say, sitting back to get a better look.

"What." Jane looks defensive, her lower jaw jutting out as if I'm about to make a nasty comment, and I realize for the first time that she's probably been putting up with nasty comments for a long time—not just from the students at Percival Lowell, but probably from the students at her own high school, too. Maybe even her junior high and grade schools. It makes sense, and it doesn't. I mean, I know Jane is kind of a wallflower, and I know she's not one to put a lot of energy into how she looks for other people, but when I look at her now I realize a genuine hottie lurks under the mop of hair and the slouchy clothes.

"Just . . . wow," I say, grinning and holding up the hand mirror so she can see for herself.

Her eyes widen a little when she looks at her reflection, and it seems like it takes her a second to realize that a face that would be considered beautiful by any sane person's standards is looking back at her.

She has a full-on smile going as I haul myself up from the couch and waddle into the kitchen to grab a pint of Ben & Jerry's and two spoons, proud of the job I've done. I'm on my way back into the living room when a third person expresses enthusiasm, too.

"Oh!" I say, stopping right in my tracks.

Jane puts the mirror down and looks at me, alarmed. "What?"

"The Bun—it kicked!"

Earl is back by New Year's Eve, and the three of us sit around at 9:45 Arizona time waiting for the ball on the television to drop in Times Square. There's a bottle of champagne for Jane and Earl and a bottle of sparkling cider for me and the Bun, and we're talking about resolutions.

"Less *Wheel of Fortune* and more *Walker, Texas Ranger,*" Earl announces, starting us off. Because, clearly, there's no such thing as too much Chuck Norris. "What about you, Janey?"

Jane bites her lower lip and looks a little shy for a second. Then she clears her throat and says, "I'm thinking about going back to my maiden name for the new year. I'm thinking about becoming Jane Greenwood again."

"Wow," I say. "No more Plain . . . you know."

She narrows her eyes at me, but she can't keep the smile off her face.

"What's your resolution, Dolores?" Earl asks from his spot next to me on the couch.

I must look completely confused, because Jane says, "That was my mom's name." Her smile changes a little, as if maybe Dolores is right here in the room with us on the last night of this crazy year, blessing our resolutions.

And I mean to say something like *My resolution is to eat healthier and get better grades this year,* but instead I blurt out, "I'm thinking about putting the baby up for adoption."

Jane and Earl just stare. The ghost of Dolores probably does, too.

"I've been trying so hard to not think about the Bun's birth," I say. And this is where I surprise all of us by getting a little teary. "But, you know, this baby is going to come, and I don't think I'm ready for it." The truth is, thoughts of what I'm going to do when the Bun is born have been trying to sneak into my head since I found out I was pregnant, and I've been doing my best to keep them out. "I know I should have thought about this sooner," I continue. "But everything is happening so fast."

I swipe a couple of tears out from under my eyes, thinking about how I might actually want to go to college and how unlikely it is that I ever will, especially with a baby. I know Jane well enough at this point to know she'd probably offer to babysit every day for me if necessary, but how is that fair? She must know what I'm thinking, because she comes over with a box of tissues and kneels down next to me. "Do you want me to help you research this?"

Earl leans over to pat my hand, and as I look down at his gnarled, reassuring fingers so gently touching my own, all I can do is nod through tears that are flowing freely now down my cheeks.

15

great expectations

THAT JANUARY is one of the coldest on record for the Southwest, so I pretty much spend the entire month inside Jane's house and my classrooms, eating and growing.

In February, for my birthday, Jane says she wants to take me shopping for maternity clothes in the next size up: "You look like you're about to bust out all your seams, Brianna."

Ever since the Christmas makeover I gave her, she's gotten into the habit of wearing a little makeup, and clothes that actually fit the figure she's been hiding for her entire adult life, but it still annoys me that all of a sudden I'm taking fashion advice from someone who's been a walking style implosion up until a couple of months ago. She's right, though, and I know it.

"I'll pay you back," I tell her, though I don't know with what money, since I'm not only huge but flat-ass broke as well.

"What are you thinking?"

"I'm thinking I should get a job is what I'm thinking."

"It's not necessary," she says. "You have enough on your plate with school and watching Earl for me. Then there's all the housecleaning you've been doing."

I sigh. "How can you be so cool about this?"

"I don't know. Maybe it's because I'm a teacher. I see a need, and I jump right in. Really, sometimes I think it's a syndrome."

"Jane, seriously. I'm eating you out of house and home."

"You can pay me back someday if you want to," she says. "But for now you need to focus on you and your baby and your education. And I just got paid, so you know what? We're going shopping."

I'm not sure why this is—probably the fluctuating hormones they warned me about at the clinic during my recent checkup—but for some reason I feel like I might start crying yet again. Maybe it's also because I've gotten so good at telling myself I don't need anything—and anything I do need I can damn well take care of myself—that any unexpected kindness knocks me off-balance. "Okay," I tell her, caving in. "But I get to pick the store."

We go to Pay-Per-Pound Thrift, where Jane talked about bringing Derek's clothes, and which happens to have been one of my favorite stores in the universe since Keisha first brought me here years ago and turned me on to the glory that is thrift store shopping.

"You can be a mall clone like every other teenybopper out there," my sister said, "or you can spend some time in the thrift stores and make your own fashion happen—fashion no single other person out there is wearing."

For good reason, I thought at the time, but once I started high school and decided to heed Jules's advice about updating my look, I realized Keisha was right. It turned out thrift store shopping wasn't just about personal style; it was also about recycling, which was cool. I bought a couple of long, flowy skirts first, tying them in knots so the fabric would drape in an interesting way across my legs. Next I paired a miniskirt with some high-tops I'd found super-cheap, and then I tried using a man's necktie as a hair band.

At first I was convinced everyone at Lowell would look at me like I was a complete freak—and maybe some of them did—but then, sure enough, I started to see people in the hallways copying me, just one or two at first, and then bunches. Before I knew it, I was officially a trendsetter.

When Jane and I start going through the racks at Pay-Per-Pound, it doesn't take me too long to find armloads of decent maternity clothes. Jane stands outside the fitting room as I try stuff on, and she tells me how each piece looks from the back when I come out. Then, returning to the racks for more, I find my treasure of the day; it's a vintage ball gown—strapless apricot satin with an overlay of cream-colored lace. It's not maternity, but right away Jane says she'll get out her sewing machine and show me how to alter it with a big panel in front to fit my "expanding frame."

"You mean my huge butt," I tell her.

"Actually, I was talking about that beer gut of yours."

Now it's my turn to stand outside the fitting room and tell Jane how things look on her when she opens the curtain and poses. And I guess I shouldn't be surprised when I glance at a mirror and see the reflection of Jules Hill standing there with a pile of clothes in her hand, because I introduced her to thrift store shopping not long after we started being friends. It was just about the only thing she was willing to admit she learned from me. And while Jules stands there staring me down and looking like she just got a whiff of spoiled milk, Jane flings open the curtain to reveal herself posing in a polka-dot dress from the sixties. "Ta-da!" she says. "Oh, hello, Jules."

Jules takes one look at the two of us and goes, "Oh my God. I mean, please."

"Whatever," I mutter under my breath.

Jane is quiet as we take our things to the counter a few minutes later. We put everything on the scale and pay our ninety-nine cents per pound, and as we're walking out to the car, Jane says, "I want to help you rearrange your school schedule."

"What are you talking about?"

"I think you should take AP English and maybe some other AP classes next semester. They'll look good on your transcript, and students in those courses are way too busy to harass each other, besides."

I just look at her. "You're kidding, right? Me. In Advanced Placement."

"No, I'm really *not* kidding, Bree," Jane says. "It will be stressful, but probably not as stressful as trying to get through my class with that kind of attitude being thrown in your face." She jerks her head back toward the store, and I know she's talking about Jules, that she finally sees what I'm up against every minute I'm at school.

"Plus," Jane says as she opens the trunk of her car so we can put our bags in there, "I can find you a tutor. Mr. Leonard, who teaches AP English, is a friend of mine."

"Seriously, Jane," I say, trying to stop her before she really gets going—which is, of course, like trying to stop a train. "Do you know who I am?"

She closes the trunk and looks at me with a mysterious smile on her face. "Do *you* know who you are?"

I don't say anything, because how is someone supposed to answer a question like that?

I stay quiet during the drive home, partly because I'm thinking about how I got to be who I am and partly because of the late-winter light turning the mountains a bright, alpenglow pink as we round a corner and the snowy Peaks come into view. After we get our bags of clothes into the house, Jane picks the conversation back up like we never stopped talking about plans for my future.

"At the very least, you need to stay in school," she says as I'm settling in at the kitchen table, getting ready to put my feet up. "So here." She hands me a list of AP classes she clearly printed out earlier, knowing full well we were going to have this conversation.

"So that's what the shopping trip was?" I demand, feeling my face get hot. "A chance for you to fix me yet again?"

"Oh, please. Get over yourself a little bit. Look. I took the liberty of circling the ones I thought would work best for you—"

"Took the *liberty,*" I mimic her under my breath, pissed off all of a sudden at how she seems to think she's just going to waltz into my life and save the day by organizing everything from my clothes to my class schedule. "Who the hell talks like that?"

For a second Jane just looks at me. Then she says, "I do. And frankly, Brianna? You can just stuff it if you don't like the way I talk." Apparently, she's pissed, too.

"Who the hell—"

"*Stuff* it, Brianna," she says again.

"I would," I say with a sarcastic smile, holding the sides of my belly. "But I'm pretty much out of places to stuff things. In case you haven't noticed."

And in that split second a shadow of the pain, fear, sadness, and rage Jane must have been feeling since the night Derek died flashes across her face. "What is it you want, exactly? Do you want me to kick you out? Is that it? Because I'm—"

"You're what?" I shout back, refusing to feel bad for her this time, because obviously I'm about to need every ounce of energy I have to take care of myself and this baby once we're homeless again. Maybe getting kicked out *is* what I want. Maybe everything's just easier that way, when I don't have to worry about what anyone else thinks or feels or how I've hurt them. "You're ready to do it? Well, go ahead, then!"

Jane doesn't say anything. Instead, she looks at me one last time, then turns around and walks down the hall, disappearing into her bedroom.

Even though I'd rather be doubled over the toilet with morning sickness again than admit Jane's right, it's not long before her idiotic idea of Brianna + AP classes = true love forever starts looking like it's actually going to work, because in early March I'm moved to the AP English class from Jane's printout. Of course, it figures it's made up almost entirely of Brain Tribe members. A few of them, Nathan Lumpke included, try to cozy up to me right off the bat, offering me Skittles and flashing their braces, but I let them know in no uncertain terms that I'm not interested.

Mr. Leonard is one of those teachers who could have been in action movies. He's handsome but tough-looking, and it's hard to believe he's single. On the wall behind his desk there are pictures of him snowboarding, white-water rafting, and skydiving. Even though he's strict and seems like someone you wouldn't want to mess with, he's cool. Example: he's never allowed any food in his classroom, but he makes a snack exception for me on my very first day, because Jane told him how things start to get dicey quick if I don't eat something like every twenty minutes. The nurse at the clinic told me it has to do with blood sugar, and I wonder if the other students are thinking *teacher's pet* or—worse—*Playne's bitch* when I pull a pb&j out of my backpack and eat the entire thing in about three bites. But it turns out they're actually pretty cool about it. For a bunch of eggheads. When Mr. Leonard asks the class if they mind, everyone says they don't, which is just bizarre. In my old English class the idiots at the back of the room would have thrown a fit: *Where's* my *snack exception?* they would have whined to Jane. *I want special treatment, too.*

So, for the moment, I make an agreement with myself not to drop out. Still, I haven't read the books on the reading list Mr. Leonard gave everyone a few weeks earlier, which means I'm completely clueless during my first week of class when all the other students are raising their hands and all but falling out of their chairs going, "Oo! Oo! I know! Pick me!" Clearly it won't be long before I hit the bottom rung of not just the social ladder but the academic ladder, too, and start leaning against the outcast railing at school—a beached whale failing all her classes and eating everything in sight.

One day Mr. Leonard says he's arranged to have me meet with a tutor during lunch.

"Okay," I say, because it's not like my social calendar is booked during that period. So the next day I'm sitting in the library, floating on a low-blood-sugar cloud (a result of not having eaten in the past thirteen minutes) and staring at some essay questions about *Great Expectations,* when someone sits down next to me. When I look up, there's Nathan Lumpke. I've managed to block out the fact that he's in my class, but here he is, smiling his big, enthusiastic smile, with what appears to be fresh pomade holding his hair helmet in place.

"Hi there, Brianna," he says.

"Oh, no," I say.

"I'm happy to see you, too. As always." He smiles again, and it occurs to me he's trying to be all rock-star-on-a-private-yacht suave. Unfortunately, it comes off more as lounge-singer-on-a-cruise-ship smarmy. Also, there's a little piece of some leafy green or other stuck between his front teeth.

"Uh, you've got something between your . . . ," I say, waving a finger in front of my teeth.

But instead of getting embarrassed or rushing to get rid of

the offending plant life, Nathan has the nerve to give me attitude. "Uh, you've got something in your . . . ," he says, waving a hand in front of his belly.

And I am completely speechless. Is this not the same Nathan Lumpke who once worshipped the ground I walked on? The same Nathan Lumpke who practically begged me to sit at the Brain Tribe table during lunch? Apparently I am now on his level—one of his kind.

He asks me what I know about Charles Dickens's novel, and when I say, "Not much," he starts lecturing me about how important it is to keep up with the reading and engage with the author's prose, and blah blah blah.

"But why does this even matter?" I ask him.

"What do you mean—AP? Why does it *matter*?"

"Yeah, Nathan. That's what I said."

"Well, college, for one," he says, perplexed. "I mean, it looks good on your records. Also, it's just—I don't know—good for your *brain*."

This goes on for a few minutes, and then, about halfway through our session, I can tell I'm losing him, because he starts answering my questions with "Uh-huh" and "Yeah" instead of his typical answers that go on forever and in way too much detail.

"Nathan, what's—" I start to say, but then I look where he's looking, and I see her. Marsha or Mildred, or something like that. I've seen her around the halls and the cafeteria, but since she only takes the advanced classes, I've never actually met her.

"Who's the hot chick?" I ask, hoping he'll get that I'm joking.

"Marjorie Kimble," he says, not even trying to sound cool.

"And your brain just turned to jelly . . . why?"

"What do you mean? Just *look* at her." His voice is all dreamy, and I wonder what kind of cheesy Muzak is playing in the background of his brain as Marjorie puts a book back on the shelf and then reaches for another one. Even with the glasses and the somewhat uneven bangs, she's not unattractive (for a brain).

Nathan just sighs.

"You're a goner," I tell him.

"What?" He allows his attention to wander back to me for a second.

"A goner," I say again. "Dead man walking."

"What are you talking about?"

"You've got it bad. That's all I'm saying."

"I'm going to ask her to prom."

The word makes my gut lurch a little. Or maybe it's the Bun kicking me in the ribs.

"Does she know?"

Nathan gets a sly smile on his face. "Oh, she knows, all right," he says. "I'm just waiting for the right moment to pop the question."

I'm stunned by how badly I want to smack him. I've been planning for my perfect first prom since I was in grade school, and here's this complete social meltdown acting like it's totally natural for someone like him to attend this incredibly important rite of passage while someone like me—someone who might have even been voted prom queen if things had turned out differently—stays home knitting baby booties, thanks to an endless supply of knitting needles and yarn in every conceivable color and texture.

16

teenager pregnant adoption how to

THOSE ARE the words I type into the search box. Even though the new AP class is killing me, I'm determined to learn as much as I can about the adoption process whenever I have a few spare minutes. Also, since I have no social life anyway, I use the next Saturday for research as well. I type in search terms until my brain is about to dribble out my ears, but I also start learning a bunch, like how you can form a relationship with the parents you choose while you're still pregnant so you can feel better about your decision. I also learn that you don't have to meet them if you don't want to, and that you can even have the baby taken away by the hospital staff before you ever get a chance to see it. That last part sounds like something I could never do, but I guess that's what some girls need—to start forgetting as soon as they can once pregnancy is over, if that's even possible.

Jane comes into the computer room after my fourth straight hour online and tilts her head to one side, studying me. "Are you sure you want to do this?" she asks.

I let out a big breath and run my fingers through my hair. "I can't remember the last time I was sure of anything," I tell her. "But yeah, I think I do."

When I turn to glance at her, she has the oddest expression on her face, like she's holding something back, something she wants to tell me but isn't sure how to do it.

"You know," she says, biting her lower lip and looking down at her hands, which are fidgeting near her stomach. "When I first found out you were pregnant, I had a crazy, insane, truly bizarre thought flash through my head."

I have absolutely no idea where Jane's headed with this, so I say nothing.

"I thought, you know, maybe I could take the baby," she says. "Adopt it, I mean, not take it like kidnap it or... You know what I mean."

I nod, speechless. Why I've never thought of it before I don't know, but it would be so perfect. I imagine the guest room transformed into a nursery, with enormous stuffed animals, a rainbow-and-clouds mural painted on the wall, and a rocking chair in the corner. Maybe I could live not too far from here and watch the baby grow up. I could be Auntie Bree....

"But it's not how I want it to go," Jane continues, smashing my fantasy to smithereens. "If I end up being a single mom someday, then okay. But it's not something I'm setting out to do. And I can hardly believe I'm saying this, because (a) you haven't offered to give me the baby—"

"But I would," I say, cutting her off. "I can't think of anyone who'd be a better—"

"And (b)," Jane says, holding up her hand to stop me from saying any more, "(b), it's just... it's not my time for this, Bree. Maybe I'm crazy. Maybe this is my last chance to hold on to a part of Derek, and I should grab it with all my might." She stops talking and looks out the window for a minute, and I swear it's like I can see the thoughts turning over and over in her mind. "You know, I've been taking care of people for a long time. Most of my life, I guess. And now I'm twenty-six, and I find myself suddenly not moving in the direction I thought I was headed. I had a husband and a job. I was going to have my own babies someday, and teach until I retired. And now... now it's like none of it was even real."

Part of me gets what she's saying. I think about how my life was going just a few short months ago. I was a cheerleader and a popular girl. I was going to break the mold, do something totally different from what my own mother did. I was going to go out into the world after high school and *be* somebody. And what ended up happening? I ended up getting pregnant at almost exactly the age Jolene was when she got pregnant with Keisha.

"Anyway," Jane is saying. She's looking at me again, and I can tell she's come back down to earth from her thought cloud. "I don't know if it started with me going back to my maiden name or you teaching me how to do my makeup, or what. But for the first time in a long time, I've actually been thinking about what it is *I* want to do. Not what I'm supposed to do or what I think people expect me to do, but what I actually want to do before I'm too old or settled down. And it turns out the list is pretty long. I want to travel. I want to take pictures. I want to maybe write a book. Of course, my dad is my priority, but I won't be much good for taking care of him if I don't start living my own life a little." She nods at the monitor, where I was typing another round of keywords when she walked in. "So I want to help you, but you need to know I'm not ready to even think about having a baby right now."

She says it almost like a kind of apology, and when her gaze shifts to my face, all I say is "It's okay, Jane. I understand." Because the truth is, as disappointed as I am, I'm also proud of her.

* * *

True to her word, Jane helps with the research whenever she can, and between the two of us we come up with a ton of information. And all of it seems like stuff that might be happening to someone else one of these days. Because even though the Bun is kicking and squirming and pushing its little feet against my insides on a regular basis by this point, a huge part of me can't even imagine what it will be like to give birth to a baby, much less to give it away.

By the end of winter, Jane and I have looked at a billion websites for a billion people wanting to adopt. There are straight couples, gay couples, vegan couples, Atkins couples, Republican couples, Democrat couples, single moms, single dads, retired grandparents, and the list goes on. We finally decide to sign up with an adoption agency, since we can at least find people who have been prescreened and background-checked that way.

Still, it isn't easy. "They all feel like dating profiles," Jane says one night when we're both totally fried from studying the agency's website, where all the couples sound so desperate to get a baby, any baby. But then, just as we're about to shut the computer down for the night, Jane stops and stares at the monitor.

"Look at this one," she says.

On the screen is a couple that looks a lot like some of the others—early-thirties-ish, nice scene in the background. Only, these people are different, and it takes me a minute to figure out why. The woman is smiling at the camera, and the man is smiling at her, and then it hits me: they aren't trying too hard. Most of the couples we've read about are working to sell themselves, to the point where their web pages look almost like online carnival games: *Step right up and pop some balloons with your virtual darts! Then meet the lovely couple who will be the perfect parents for your baby!*

"Craig and Rose," I read aloud from their profile. "I like them."

"They don't seem so high-pressure," Jane says, scanning their bio. "Plus, good job, nice house, good relationship with the grandparents. And I like what they say about believing the right match will happen in its own time."

I sit back in my chair and let out a big, slow breath. "I want to meet them."

After the necessary arrangements have been made, Jane drives me down to Tempe—which is a few hours south of us—and we introduce ourselves to Craig and Rose Gilbert. Jane doesn't want to be in the way during our meeting, so she excuses herself and tells me she'll be back in a couple of hours.

"My favorite mall is right near here," she explains to the Gilberts, and I just look at her like her eyebrows have spontaneously burst into flame. Because even though she's started pulling her style together lately, anyone who looks at Jane for more than two seconds can see that the idea of someone like her having a favorite mall is absurd. It's like a nun having a favorite lingerie boutique.

The Gilberts invite me into their living room, where they both sit up so straight on the couch that it looks like they might give me a military salute at any moment. And I have to keep myself from staring at their hands, which are intertwined so closely that it's hard to tell who's holding on tighter. It's almost like they're trying to anchor each other to the couch, and to keep myself from getting too on edge, I just start talking.

I tell them about what happened with me and Derek, and I tell them what happened with Keisha and Jules, and about how I ended up at Hope House. Then I tell them about Jane and how she took me in.

When I'm done, I look at the two of them. They aren't saying anything, but Rose looks like she might be about to cry.

"I'm sorry," I say. "Was that . . . too much information?"

And that's when Rose does cry. A tear slips down her cheek,

and she wipes it away with a tissue Craig hands her from a box on the coffee table.

"You poor thing," she says to me. "This must be the hardest thing you've ever done."

I don't know what to say in response, so instead I just file her comment away in a far corner of my brain, look both of them in the eye, and say, "So, tell me about you guys."

Craig clears his throat. "Well, for starters," he says, "I think we can relate to a lot of the heartache you've been talking about."

Is that what it is? I wonder. *Heartache?* Because I've been thinking it was just my punishment for getting to be one of the lucky ones—a popular cheerleader who never deserved to be where she was but who got there anyway and then threw it all away in a single night. As Mo told me the first day at Hope House, there's always a price to pay.

"We had a child," Craig says, interrupting my thoughts. "It was about two years ago. But, um . . ." He clears his throat again and looks down for a second. When he looks back up at me, there are tears in his eyes, too. "There were complications, and he passed away when he was about twelve hours old."

"He was our little guy," Rose says, patting her husband's hand.

"I don't really know what to say," I tell them. I try to swallow the lump in my throat, but it isn't going anywhere.

"Anyway," Rose says, wiping her eyes again and smiling at me. "After that, the doctors told us there was a genetic issue, and we shouldn't even try to have more children. I was devastated. Just a total wreck."

"You're way too modest," Craig tells her. "You're the strongest person I've ever known."

She waves his comment away but squeezes his hand and continues. "So I just sort of figured, you know, that we'd never have kids. I never even thought about adoption, because I guess I felt it was so important to have a child of our own. But then, about a year ago, I started to think maybe I had it all wrong. Maybe Craig and I were meant to be parents after all, just not the way I'd always thought it was going to be. Do you get what I mean?"

"I think I do," I tell her.

Talking about this stuff is tiring, and Craig provides a break by making lunch for us, and then we sit around and talk some more, which is when I remember something.

"You don't have to worry about having the baby's heart checked," I tell them, swallowing a bit of my sandwich. "I mean, if you end up being the parents. Derek's—the dad's—heart issues weren't something that could be passed on." Part of me can't believe I'm actually using the word "dad" to talk about Derek, but let's face it—that's what he is. Was. Then I just sit there and look at them, feeling like an idiot and wondering if I should have maybe eased into that memo a little bit first.

"Brianna," Craig says. He looks into my eyes and holds my gaze, and I think *Now you've blown it, Bree. You should never have said "baby" and "heart issues" in the same sentence. He's going to tell you they're not interested, that they've already had enough baby health heartache to last a lifetime.*

But that's not what Craig says at all. Instead, he glances quickly at his wife and says, "I think I can speak for both Rose and myself when I say that, when something is meant to be, there's no need to worry."

During the rest of the visit I learn more about them, like the fact that Craig is an architect and Rose was a cheerleader in high school, just like me.

"We didn't do all the crazy stuff they do now, though," she says, shaking her head. "I don't know how you could ever launch yourself through the air like that."

I help clear the dishes, and it's in the kitchen that I realize *Here is where the Bun will eat his or her first cereal. Over there next to the sink is where his or her bottles will dry on the wash rack.* For some reason, this is the room that brings it all home. I try to figure out if I'm sad or scared or freaked out at the thought of my baby—the little human growing less little every day in my belly—here in this house, three hours away from me. But I'm none of those things. It's a good house, a good kitchen, and these are good people. It's just . . . a little weird to think about.

There's a knock at the door. Rose leaves the kitchen and then comes back with Jane, who's back from the trip to her "favorite mall." Jane looks at me carefully, to see if I'm handling the situation okay, and I give a slight nod as we follow Craig and Rose toward the entry hall.

Rose gives me a hug before we leave. "You're a special young woman, Brianna. Thank you so much for coming to meet us."

When I turn to say good-bye to Craig, he says, "I don't know about you, but for me there's just something that feels right about this."

I nod again, more fully this time, but I don't tell him what I'm thinking, which is *I totally agree.* And as Jane and I walk back to her car in silence, a couple more things occur to me: Rose just might be the kind of mother I've always wished for, and Craig just might be one of those good guys who have seemed so rare to me all my life.

When Jane and I get back in her car and head toward home, my brain is so full of details from my visit with the two people I've already decided are going to be the Bun's parents that it takes me about twenty miles to say out loud what I'm feeling. It's not until we're back on I-17, heading north toward Flagstaff, that I say, "I feel so lucky to have found them."

"Yeah," Jane says, looking out the driver's-side window, out across the tan Sonoran desert. "But they're the really lucky ones, you know. Because they found you, too."

And right there I wonder how it could have taken me so long to see how beautiful Jane really is. I was always so fixated on her bad fashion sense and the fact that she never did anything with her face or her hair. And I could never figure out what Derek saw in her. I mean, he was so cute and funny, and she was—well, she was Plain Jane, for crying out loud.

But when she tells me Craig and Rose were lucky to find me, I know two things for a fact: (1) She's serious, which makes it mean more to me than almost anything anyone has told me before; and (2) I still have a lot of growing up to do. Because I don't care how unnecessarily fugly Jane lets herself get sometimes. Let's face it: she deals with a bunch of high school Neanderthals every day and then goes back home to take care of her dad. The simple truth is that even if she had the head of an aye-aye and the body of a blobfish (go ahead, look them up), any man would be crazy not to fall in love with someone like her.

Nathan Lumpke starts helping me study for the AP exam in late March, because even though exams won't be held for over a month, the clinic nurse said you never know what might happen in the last two months of pregnancy when you're my age.

It's gotten to where I have to sit like two feet back from the library table when we're working after school and rest the book on my belly, which now looks more like a beach ball stuffed under my maternity shirt than an actual part of my body. Also, I'm exhausted all the time now, since the Bun has decided to become a night owl and practice womb gymnastics while I'm trying to sleep—and there's no way to get comfortable when you have a tiny person using your bladder as a trampoline.

Nathan seems distracted today, too, and to snap us both back into reality, I say, "So. Did she say yes?"

Nathan jumps a little. "Huh?"

"Huh?" I say, mimicking him with a little spazzy hand gesture. "Marjorie. You know, love of your life, blah blah blah. Did she say yes when you asked her to prom?"

"Oh," Nathan says, looking down. "Yeah."

"Big surprise," I say, stifling a burp the Bun must have jogged loose.

"But we're not going."

I just look at him. Oh, the mysteries of geekdom. "Okay, Nate. I'll bite. What's going on?" I call him Nate now, even though he told me nobody else calls him that, not even his parents.

Nate glances at me and then back down at his hands. "Something sort of just . . . happened," he says.

"*What* sort of just happened?"

"Jules Hill."

There are no words.

"She just started working at Ye Olde Prom Shoppe in the mall, and she totally came on to me when I went to rent my tux."

"Jules Hill," I say, gradually getting my voice back. "Came on to you."

"Yes! Jules Hill! You know, red-hot cheerleader with the"—Nate cups his hands out in front of his chest—"and the"—he leans forward and cups them behind his butt.

"Okay, I get it," I say, holding a hand up because there is no way to un-see any of what he just did. "You can stop now."

"Anyway, Jules said, 'Who are you going with?' and I said, 'Marjorie Kimble,' and Jules said, 'Seriously? Because I don't have a date.' "

"Yeah, right," I say, rolling my eyes. Because if I know Jules, she's probably had ten football players lined up since the beginning of the school year, just so she could pick and choose when the time came.

"I know!" Nate says, getting really into retelling the story. "I said, 'Jules, I'm sure someone will ask you. Like the whole football team, for example.' And do you know what she said?"

"Surprise me."

"She said . . ." Here Nate has to stop and swallow before he speaks again, because he's getting a little emotional. "She said, 'I hope it's someone as sweet as you.' "

"Aww," I say, rolling my eyes until my sockets actually hurt. "That is *so* cute." At the same time, though, I'm wondering what Jules is thinking. And then it hits me: Nathan Lumpke has replaced Jane as this year's victim. I know it the way I know I'll have to get up at least twice in the middle of the night tonight to pee. I think back to the Monday after Derek died, when Nate stood in front of me and Jules in the hallway, all big-eyed and shaky, only to get laughed off. Jules always did have a special knack for torturing him.

"Seriously, Nate," I say. "Did the fact that you've already asked Marjorie to the prom slip your mind?"

"No, it didn't. But after Jules said what she said about me being sweet, I just . . . I told Marjorie and the others that we should all just go in a big group, and that we shouldn't have dates at all."

"Okay, then. If that's how you brains roll."

Nate takes a deep breath. "And then I went back into Ye Olde Prom Shoppe and asked Jules to go with me."

I can't believe what I'm hearing. "Wait. You what?"

"I mean, I *like* Marjorie and everything—"

"Get out of here, Nate," I tell him, slapping my pencil down on the table and hearing a "*Shhhh!*" come from the librarian's desk. "You *worship* Marjorie."

"No, Brianna," he says, looking me straight in the eye so I know he's serious. "I worship Jules. I have since the first day of freshman year."

"Um, news flash," I hiss, looking around to see if the librarian's about to bust me for being too loud again. "But you don't dump the woman of your dreams to go out with a total—"

"A total what?"

"Never mind," I say, releasing my irritation in one big sigh.

Just then, Nate's phone rings, making me jump. "My ringtone's the TIE fighter theme from *Star Wars,*" he says, looking bashful and pleased with himself as he answers.

"Hey," he says. I fear it might be Jules on the other end, and my stomach is in no way ready to handle a shmookie-wookie conversation between Nathan Lumpke and Jules Hill.

"I'll let her know. Bye, Ms. Playne—I mean Greenwood."

"Jane?" I ask as he puts the phone back in its belt-clip holster.

"Yeah. She just wanted me to tell you that she's really sorry, but she can't go to Lamaze class with you tonight. She has to stay late for a parent-teacher conference that got rescheduled at the last minute, so she wants me to drive you home."

"Okay," I say. And then, because Nate is staring at me with his mouth open, clearly confused, I add, "Lamaze is a childbirth class."

Blank stare.

"For empowering pregnant ladies? You know," I say, imitating the breathing Jane and I learned during the first class. "*Hee hee hoo?* I'm learning stuff that's supposed to make labor easier. Jane's my coach."

"So what are you going to do?"

"Go alone. No bigs."

"But it sounds like you need a partner, right?"

I shrug, too tired to think about it all of a sudden. "I don't know. Maybe I just won't go."

He puts down his pen. "Let me go with you."

"No, Nate."

"Why not?"

"Because you're an idiot," I tell him. "Because you threw away the chance to go to prom with a girl who is perfect for you, all because of somebody like Jules."

"Weren't you two friends?"

"Just do yourself a favor and watch your back," I say, ignoring the question.

"What's that supposed to mean?"

"I don't know. Jules is just... God, never mind. You are *not* coming to my Lamaze class, and that's final."

"Okay, fine," Nate says, crossing his arms in front of his chest. "Go alone, then. Don't let me drive you. Or better yet, don't go at all. I'm sure you won't need that breathing or anything when you're giving birth to an actual *person*."

An hour later, the two of us are walking into one of the rooms at the community center, no doubt getting all kinds of stares from the pregnant ladies and their coaches huddled together on mats scattered throughout the room. Not that I actually see those stares, because there's no way I'm going to look anyone in the face. In the car on the way over here Nate cranked up a 1980s AM radio station ("This is my favorite Devo song!") and then slicked his hair back with a little black comb he pulled from his shirt pocket. He's a distracted driver anyway, and I had to restrain myself from grabbing the steering wheel to make sure we didn't run off the road. Then, after parking his ancient Volkswagen Bug, he rolled his socks all the way down. ("A nervous habit," he told me, "for when I'm facing an unknown situation.") The socks are like white donuts around his ankles now, and I want to stand in the front of the room and make a general announcement to the other moms-to-be: *Just in case you all are wondering, this guy is* not *the baby daddy.*

It turns out he's not a bad Lamaze coach, though. While the instructor is wandering around the room correcting couples' techniques, Nate's right there encouraging me like he's been doing *hee-hoo* breathing his whole life. He's almost like a . . . dare I even think it? . . . like a really enthusiastic, *really* homely cheerleader.

17

someone to miss

KEISHA CALLS ME out of the blue in early April. When the phone rings I'm sitting on my bed looking over the adoption contract that came in the mail the day before from the Gilberts' lawyer.

"Robby's gone," she says when I ask her how she's doing. "For good."

I don't know whether to say "Sorry" or "Finally," so instead I just say, "Oh."

"He turned out to be kind of a loser."

This time, I hold my tongue completely.

"So how far along are you?"

"Almost eight months," I tell her.

"Are you going to keep it?" Leave it to Keisha to come right out and ask something like that after we haven't spoken for eons.

"I don't know yet," I tell her, lying. For some reason I don't want to mention Craig and Rose Gilbert.

"Jolene doesn't think you will," Keisha says. "She thinks you'll cave and give the kid up for adoption because you're not tough like she was at your age. I just said, 'Whatever, Jolene.' "

Even though I try not to let them, those words still sting.

"Anyway," Keisha is saying, "I think you should definitely keep it."

She says some other stuff, too, but I don't really hear what it is, because all of a sudden all I can think about is how good it would feel once and for all to show Jolene that she no longer has the power to wreck my life with a single comment. I may be a kid still, but that's only going to last for another year. By this time next year, I'll be eighteen, and I'll damn well show her that I'm not only smart enough to raise this baby on my own, but I'm tough and independent enough, too. I feel these things so strongly—like a fire in my chest—that for a second I think maybe I've said them out loud.

Keisha doesn't seem to notice anything different in my voice, though, and she keeps going on about how great it would be to have a niece she could spoil. Finally, I tell her I have to go, and I hang up the phone.

I pick it back up almost immediately and dial the phone number on the contract, the one on the line next to *Adoptive Parents: Craig and Rose Gilbert*.

Rose picks up on the first ring. "Brianna! We were just unboxing the crib we bought today. Let me get Craig on the line, too."

I hear her call him, and then Craig is there on the phone with us. "Hi, Brianna," he says. "We got our contract from our attorney yesterday. Did you get yours yet?"

"Yeah, I did."

"We're so excited, Bree," Rose says. "You should see the baby's room. Since we don't know if it's a boy or a girl yet, Craig picked up some pale green paint—Forest Mist, I think it's called. Right, honey? Anyway—"

"You guys, I need to tell you something," I say, cutting Rose off before either of them can say another word about paint or cribs or contracts. "There's been a change of plans."

"I don't understand," Rose says. Then, more quietly, "Craig, can you come into this room, please? Wait, Brianna. I want him with me."

I hear the click of Craig's line when he hangs up, and then a few seconds later Rose says, "Okay, we're listening."

I tell them I don't think I can go through with it, that I've given the whole adoption thing a lot of thought and I don't think it's going to be the right thing for me or the baby.

It's clear they can hear the doubt in my voice, though, because Craig says, "Are you really sure about this, Brianna? Because you honestly don't sound sure."

What I think is *How could I possibly be sure?* What I say is "I am sure."

"Is it something we did?" Rose cries. "Something we said?" And I can hear Craig in the background, trying to calm her down, trying to hold the pieces of her breaking heart together.

So this is how it feels to be the rejecter, I think. It occurs to me that I've probably rejected a lot of people over the years—people like Nathan Lumpke and his friends, people I thought didn't matter, people I saw as somehow lower than me on the social ladder. For some reason I never realized how talented I was at doing it until now, and that realization leaves a sick feeling in the pit of my stomach, right above where the Bun sits curled and waiting to make its big debut.

"Please," Rose says before the call ends, begging through her tears. "Please . . . just call us if you change your mind."

I must finally be tired of how much secrets weigh. I must not be strong enough to carry them for any length of time anymore, because I tell Jane what I did as soon as she gets home from her faculty meeting that night. I expect her to be sad or angry with me, but instead she just gets really quiet.

"Are you sure?" she asks finally, echoing Craig's words.

I nod. All I know is that it's done now, and I'm going to have my chance to show Jolene and the rest of the world how tough and independent I really am.

"Well, you're basically an adult now, Brianna," Jane says. "And it's your decision to make. I'm sure you know what you're doing."

I nod again, but this time I have to swallow away the lump in my throat. It would have been easier if she had broken down into tears like Rose or yelled at me for making yet one more stupid mistake. It would have been easier if she had just kicked me out.

Just before dinnertime that Friday evening, Jane, Earl, and I walk a couple of blocks to a park where there are trees and picnic tables by a little creek. It's the weekend of prom, but instead of getting my nails done and setting everything out for tomorrow, I'm here—a pregnant ex-cheerleader in the company of an English teacher wearing farmer overalls and an old man who thinks he's living in the days of the horse and buggy. *Quite the A-list,* I'm thinking.

Jane has brought a picnic dinner, and while I look around for the outdoor bathrooms, she lays everything out on a table beneath a giant oak tree.

"Such a beautiful place," Earl says when I return. He tips his fedora to a woman in expensive-looking spandex and running shoes as she jogs past.

"It is beautiful," Jane agrees, unwrapping cold cuts and arranging them on a plate. I can tell she's watching me out of the corner of her eye, too, because she's been doing it ever since I told her about my call to Craig and Rose.

Turning to me, Earl says, "Let's come back here soon, Dolores."

"Dad," Jane says, setting the cold cuts down and putting one of her hands on his. "That's Brianna. She lives with us, remember?"

"Oh, yes, yes," Earl says, placing one of his hands on mine. "You're a charming girl."

And I have to wonder if it does any good—Jane trying to set her dad straight when he is clearly slipping more and more into his own fantasy world. It seems to me it would be better to just let him hang out there with his beloved Dolores.

I wake up for about half a second the next morning when I hear Jane heading out the door to run errands. Then I fall back to sleep for another few hours, and when I wake up, my entire right side is numb. Since I'm basically little more than a baby house at this point, I have only two possible sleeping positions—right side and left side. Lying on my stomach is like lying across a small boulder, and it also feels like I'm squashing the Bun. Lying on my back feels like a boulder is squashing *me,* and I've also heard it cuts off the baby's blood supply. So, with my eyes still closed, I brace my hands on my belly and roll over as carefully as I can to my left side.

Half an hour later, when I realize I'm never going to get comfortable, I head down to the kitchen to get some cereal. I expect to see Earl sitting at the table as usual, dressed and combed and smelling like some old-fashioned aftershave, but he's not there. I notice his bedroom door is open, though, so I peek inside. Nothing. Nobody. He's not in the recliner, either.

And then I notice that Earl's fedora is not hanging on its hook by the kitchen door, which is where he always keeps it when he's home.

I call Jane on her cell. "Earl's not here. Is he with you?"

Silence at first. Then her voice, fearful and quiet: "No."

"Don't worry," I tell her. "I'm sure he's around here somewhere." Like Earl is a set of keys that's been misplaced.

"I'm calling the police," Jane says. I hear the strain in her voice, imagine a gray streak appearing like magic in her hair.

"Don't, Jane. I'll find him. Everything is going to be okay." And I can't remember the last time I've said that out loud; it feels like I'm speaking a foreign language.

Then I remember what Earl said last night at the park: "Such a beautiful place. . . . Let's come back here soon."

Sure enough, after waddling as fast as I can for a few blocks—cradling my belly the whole way—that's where I find him. He's standing next to the picnic table where we ate our dinner, and he's staring straight up through the leaves of the giant oak to where huge puffy clouds are moving fast overhead on a late-spring breeze.

"Looking for a nest?" I ask, approaching him slowly. Part of me is afraid that, in his confusion, he might bolt. At this point I'm not sure who would outrun who, but what a sight we'd be. I can see the online video title now: "Pregnant Teen Chases Senile Geezer." It would probably get a billion hits.

"Dolores," he says, turning around and beaming at me. "I've been waiting for you."

Again with the Dolores stuff, I think. But what I say out loud is "I'm here."

"The music is so beautiful in the treetops," Earl says. "Can you hear it? They're playing our song, sugarplum."

"Our song," I say. "Right." I play along the best I can.

"Dance with me," Earl says, and I freeze. "Please, my dear. I've gussied up just for this occasion."

I have to admit, Earl does look a little fancier than usual this morning. His hair is slicked back with the Dax wax Jane buys for him online, and he's wearing his starched Sunday shirt.

"Just one dance," he says. "And then it's time for church."

"I—I . . . ," I say. Then I give up, let out a sigh, and step toward him with my arms held out.

Earl's face lights up, and I realize what nice teeth he has for an old guy. He must have been quite a catch back in the day, and I wonder if Jane's mom knew how lucky she was to have someone love her so much. Probably she did, which is why he misses her as much as he does.

"I'm a little rusty," I tell him.

"Not to worry, my dear. Not to worry. It's just a waltz. Nothing to get bamboozled by." Earl raises one of his arms to his side and rounds out the other, giving me a frame to work with. I know enough to place my hand on his higher one and to let his other hand rest on my waist—what's left of my waist, anyway.

He's surprisingly graceful. "*One* two three, *One* two three," he counts quietly while guiding me in a slow circle, and I don't even bother staring down toward my feet to make sure I'm getting the steps right, because I haven't been able to see my feet for weeks.

Earl is still beaming, nodding his encouragement. "Splendid," he tells me. Then he glances down at my bulging belly. "You may, however, want to cut down on the sweets a bit, darling."

"I'm pregnant, Earl. Remember?"

"Well, congratulations! But it's no matter. You're a lovely girl despite the appetite. My beautiful Dolores."

Sigh.

Even though it makes me happy to be able to do this simple thing for him, I also feel sad. I'm sad more for me than for Earl, though, because he's lucky enough to have someone to miss. I've never had anyone like that, unless you count the imaginary father I created in my head when I was a little kid. And the truth is, I'm not sure I ever will have my own someone to love so much that I call him into existence even after he's long gone.

I don't have too long to be sad about this before Earl switches realities as only Earl can do. "I always thought Janey could do better," he says out of the blue.

So we're talking about Derek now, I think.

"That guy turned out to be about as useful as tits on a boar, dying on Janey like he did."

"I like to say 'windshield wipers on a submarine,'" I tell him, proud of myself for not missing a beat, even if it feels a little morbid to be talking about Derek's death this way. Carefully, I ease us out of the waltz and back to a normal walking rhythm.

"Heh," Earl says as I gently take him by the elbow and guide him toward the road home. "I'll have to remember that one. I was on a submarine, you know."

"Really? Tell me all about it." I try to look as interested as possible to keep him focused, but I'm all but grinding my teeth at the stress of wanting to get back home so I can call Jane and tell her I found her father.

Oblivious to the fact that he almost caused two heart attacks in a single day, Earl goes to bed before sunset that evening. "Time to toddle off to Lullaby Land!" he says like the chirpy songbird he is, kissing the top of Jane's head and then the top of mine before shuffling down the hall to his room.

Meanwhile, Jane and I just sit there staring at the kitchen table, both of us so exhausted from the adrenaline surge of thinking we'd lost him that we seem to have lost the ability to form simple words instead. Jane has big bags under her eyes that make her look about a hundred, and I'm so fried I've completely forgotten that it's prom night.

Until the doorbell rings.

"Don't move," Jane says, knowing that it takes about five minutes for me to get up from a chair at this point. I'm as bad as Earl trying to get out of his recliner. "I'll go see who it is."

A minute later she comes back into the kitchen, followed by Nathan Lumpke, of all people. It figures. Because it's not like the day has been hallucinogenic enough.

"The hell, Nate," I say, frowning at him. He looks nervous and embarrassed to be standing there with the two of us in our bathrobes while he's dressed to the nines in a pastel-blue tuxedo that must have come from Eddie's House of Lounge Lizard Apparel. Oh, wait. It came from an even cheesier place—Ye Olde Prom Shoppe, where my good buddy Jules Hill works. I start to chuckle a little, until it occurs to me that I should probably cut him some slack for a change. That's a hard thing to do even when I'm well rested, though.

Nate doesn't seem to notice that he's about to be laughed at. Instead, he hands me a clear plastic clamshell box with a lavender-colored rose corsage inside. "I know I don't deserve it," he says. "But you'd be doing me a huge favor."

I look from Nate to Jane, who's sitting in her chair again, just shrugging. "Okay, I am totally not following you," I tell him.

"I think he needs a prom date," Jane says, like Nate isn't standing right there with us. She says it the same way she'd say *Please pass the salt,* as if nothing could possibly surprise her at this point.

"You don't even have to be my date per *se*," Nate says, and all of a sudden it sounds like he's trying to sell me something. "I just need your help."

"Why?"

"Because Jules dumped me."

I open my mouth to speak. I don't know what I'm going to say—*I told you so* or *Poor baby* or *Well, duh*—but it doesn't matter because Nate beats me to the punch.

"No, let me rephrase that," he says. "Jules never really intended to go with me in the first place. I feel so stupid. I've officially been plunked."

"Punk'd," I correct him with an irritated sigh. "God, Nate. It's not like that's really a surprise. I don't know why you came here. You should have called Marjorie."

"That's why I need your help. She won't have anything to do with me. Besides, they're all going as one big group like I told them to. They all hate me."

And before I can block it from my cerebral cortex, there it is—an image of the entire Brain Tribe, all dressed up in their floor-length dresses and Easter-egg-colored tuxedos, huddled together on the dance floor, not looking anyone in the eye but trying to find the music's rhythm despite the fact that they all no doubt dance like they're being Tasered.

"We'll see about that," I tell him. Because what Nate doesn't know is that I've seen Marjorie looking at him exactly the same way he looks at her. I saw it that first day after he took a break from staring at her in the library, and I've seen it in the hallways and in the classroom when Nate's been so lost in the maze of algebraic equations or sentence diagrams in his head that he's totally oblivious to anything else. And Marjorie might be different from me (a separate species, even), but I still recognize the Look a girl gets when she's got it bad for a guy (assuming that's what Nate is, of course). Not that I've ever bothered to point out Marjorie's obvious mutual feelings to him, because let's be real: even if I wasn't already a total social leper, I am *so* not going into business as a matchmaker for the Academic Decathlon set.

But then again, Nate is my friend.

"This is against my better judgment, and we are totally even for the whole stand-in Lamaze coach thing now" is all I say. "Big-time." I hold out my hand so he can haul me out of the kitchen chair, and I tell him to put the corsage in the fridge to keep it fresh, but not to take it out of its case. After rolling my eyes at him, I tromp up the stairs as loudly as I can so he'll get just how annoyed I am. Turns out this is no challenge whatsoever, since I weigh about half a ton.

Upstairs in my room I rummage around in the closet until I find the apricot satin dress Jane bought for me at Pay-Per-Pound. I take it off the hanger and hold it out so I can get a good look. Then I call down to Jane to please come upstairs and help me put it on.

18

boof, my pelvis goes

TWENTY MINUTES LATER, after I take my life in my hands by getting into Nate's thirty-year-old car yet again, the two of us—three, if you count the Bun—head up the steps in front of the downtown hotel where prom is being held. There's a little table set up in the lobby, and Ms. Grimes is standing there with a camera.

"I'm the paparazzi tonight!" she says, clearly pleased with herself and pointing to a bench surrounded by flowers, balloons, and glittery streamers. Apparently, Nate and I are supposed to sit there with our arms around each other, grinning and posing.

Then Grimes turns back toward us and sees that nobody is smiling here.

"Oh," she says, glancing at my belly. "Maybe we'll just take a head shot."

"No pictures," I say.

"Yeah," Nate says, taking my elbow and guiding me toward the two big doors though which music is spilling out with a bass line so loud I can feel it—as Jules might poetically say—in my crotch. "It's our policy."

I glance at him and smile. He might actually make a good sidekick with some training.

Once we're inside the ballroom, Jules is the first person I see. She's wearing a tiara and a big purple sash that says QUEEN, and across the room I can see Braden Lewis in his prom king crown and robe, laughing with the other football players as they all shove each other around. I imagine Grimes just about coming unhinged with joy at the thought of doing an entire photo shoot with Jules and Braden out there in the lobby.

"Congratulations," I tell Jules as we pass her.

"Nice dress," she says in response, sneering first at my midsection and then at Nate, who stands there in the Presence like a deflated balloon, looking at the floor. "Nice . . . everything."

Sarcasm noted, I think as she walks away. *Bitch.* I continue to smile, though, because why let her know she got to me?

Kimmy and Charlotte are watching us from the other side of the room, but when I raise my hand to wave hello, they both look away quickly. And I actually pity them a little at that moment for not being strong enough to stand up to someone like Jules, someone who uses spineless wonders like they are to make herself feel superior. I should know: I was once spineless, too.

"Oh, boy, there she is," Nate says, and I look over to where he's staring: at the far corner of the ballroom Marjorie is standing with a bunch of other Brain Tribe representatives, and all of them are ignoring Nate completely. I think I see Marjorie sneak a look our way, but then she turns so her back is toward us.

At least he got over Jules's nasty comment pretty quickly, I think—probably because he's had a lot of practice over the years. Still, I feel a little pang in my chest on his behalf, because I know all too well that feeling of being shunned by people you thought were your friends.

Beside me, Nate starts to tremble as he says, "I'm not sure I'm ready for this."

And that's when I reach into my bag and take out the plastic clamshell, which I grabbed from the fridge before we left Jane's house. I hand it to Nate with strict orders: "Keep this behind your back, and when she comes over here, tell her you have something for her."

"She's not coming anywhere near me, Brianna."

"Shut up and listen," I say. "Tell her you're an idiot, that you don't know what you were thinking asking someone like Jules to prom. Tell Marjorie she's the girl for you and nobody else even comes close."

"Wha—" Nate says, clearly confused.

I grab his shoulders and give them a little shake. "You know, for a smart guy, you can be pretty simple-minded. You're about to get your girl back, you dope. Close your mouth."

I walk toward the group of Nate's friends, and I can't help looking at the pastel prom dresses with poufy sleeves that might have been cutting-edge circa 1985 and think how accurate my vision of about an hour earlier was. *Oh, the horror,* I think. Then it occurs to me that I'm not really one to talk, since I look like a vintage hot-air balloon.

"Hey, Marjorie," I say, walking up behind her. I can tell she doesn't want to look at me, and I don't blame her, because I can only imagine how all of this must look—me showing up with the guy who was supposed to be her date.

"Uh, can we help you?" It's Charlie Donovan, the clear leader of the Brain Tribe, who's standing there staring me down. The other members of the tribe have arranged themselves in front of Marjorie like she needs protection, and they're all focused on trying to intimidate me with their laser eyes.

"Look, I just have a quick favor to ask her," I half-shout over the music, trying to show them all that I'm no threat.

"A favor?" Charlie repeats.

"It's okay, guys," Marjorie says, stepping out from behind her friends. "Let her talk."

"Okay," I say, and all of a sudden I'm nervous—nervous on Nate's behalf, because if Marjorie rejects me, she'll be rejecting him, too. This is my chance to make sure that doesn't happen, though, and I'm not about to blow it. "I know you don't want to forgive Nathan," I tell her. "Just—please—give him one more chance."

"I don't think that's—" she starts to say, her eyes and voice flatter, even, than her chest (yes, I went there), but I cut her off.

"Just look at him, Marjorie. I know he hurt you, but believe me, he's suffered."

Which is, of course, what the small, vengeful part of any girl who's ever been unfairly dumped and publicly humiliated wants to hear. We both look over at Nate, who, sure enough, is standing there looking like a basset hound that's just been swatted with a rolled-up newspaper for peeing on the carpet.

"Aw," Marjorie says, getting that dreamy look I've seen before in her eyes, the one that was always wasted on Nate because he was so oblivious.

Fortunately, he isn't oblivious now. Instead, his eyes lock on to Marjorie's across the dance floor, and he stares at her for a few seconds before mouthing the words that cause her to walk away from the rest of the tribe and toward him: *I. Am. So. Sorry.*

By this point I have to pee so badly I'd just about settle for a carpet myself. The bass isn't just reverberating in my crotch now; it's traveling all the way to my sternum. On my way to the restroom I turn and look back. Marjorie and Nate are facing each other. She has her eyes closed and her palms up, and she's smiling ever so slightly.

Nice touch, Nate, I think with a smile as he places the plastic clamshell with the corsage inside on her palms. *Maybe I should be* your *sidekick.*

I push open the door of the restroom, and my eyes have to adjust to two things: (1) the sudden bright light, and (2) Jules, Kimmy, and Charlotte standing at the long counter just inside the doorway, fixing their makeup and giggling like crazed hyenas. Kimmy and Charlotte freeze when they see me in the mirror, but Jules just smiles and turns around with a look Nate would describe as *Now, young Skywalker, you will die.*

"Oh my God," she says, stepping toward me so that we'd be almost nose to nose if it wasn't for the Bun. "What are you even thinking, Bree? I mean seriously, what do you have to say for yourself?"

And all I want to do at that point is get right back in her face and say, *What the hell is your problem? What did I ever do to you?*

"What—" I start to answer, but I don't finish the sentence. Instead, I look down as something inside my pelvis shifts not just in an unfamiliar way but in a way that makes a sound.

Boof, my pelvis goes, and the next thing I know, a gallon of fluid is gushing out of my womb, soaking my dress and splashing all over the Jimmy Choos Jules no doubt borrowed from her mom.

Nate and Marjorie are sitting on either side of me in the taxi, and as we head to the hospital he tries to get me to breathe.

"Hee hee hoo!" he practically shouts. "Remember, Brianna? *Hee hee hoo!*"

I do my best to follow along, but I must be doing it wrong, because as I look up and see the taxi driver's worried eyes in the rearview mirror, things start going all sparkly, and I feel like I'm about to pass out.

"We should call somebody," Marjorie says, getting her cell phone out of her purse.

"Call—" I start to say, but I don't say anything more, because right there in the taxi I have one of those moments of total mental clarity: there is no regret and no fear. In that moment I don't wish I had the kind of mother who would tell me what to do. I don't even wish I had a father whose name or phone number I knew. I don't wish anything. Instead, I simply know that Jane and Earl, Nate, and now Marjorie—all the people who have shown up during the past nine months and caught me when I stumbled and picked me up when I fell flat on my face—all those people might not look like much from the outside (maybe they're a little plain, maybe a little senile and/or geeked out), but to me they look like family.

Finally, I manage to get the words out just as the first serious contraction hits. "Call . . . *Jaaaaaaaaane!*" Then, when that gut-wrenching pain is done, I have just enough breath left to recite Jane's number and say, "This isn't real. This can't be happening."

Marjorie starts punching the keypad of her phone with the speed and accuracy of someone who's won more than one calculator race, and Nate switches into total analytical rocket scientist mode. "It would appear that it is happening despite that fact," he says.

On top of being breathless, I'm also cold and shivery all of a sudden, and all I can think to say is "Shut up, Nate!"

Marjorie shoots him a look, too. "I'm not getting an answer," she says in her soft voice, "but I'll keep trying." Then she snaps her phone shut and squeezes my hand. "What's wrong, Brianna? I mean, aside from the obvious."

"I'm not supposed to be having the baby yet. I'm early!"

"How early?"

"Like a month."

"It's going to be okay," she says, squeezing my hand a little harder. "It's going to be okay." But I catch her looking nervously at Nate when she thinks I'm not watching.

"It *is* going to be okay," the nurse assures me, echoing Marjorie's words as she folds up the footrests of a wheelchair inside the ER waiting room so I don't trip on them. "It's not unusual for babies to come early with young mothers. You're going to be fine."

Another contraction hits as she helps lower me into the chair, and I hold on to the armrests for dear life while I cry out *"Guuuuuuh!"* When the contraction ends, I glance over at Nate and Marjorie, who are standing near the waiting room seats. They're clutching each other in their outdated formal wear, both of them wide-eyed and looking like they took a serious wrong turn on their way to prom. But they're perfect for each other, and as a commercial for chewable antacid tablets plays on the television above their heads, it occurs to me that I missed my true calling: I *should* have been a matchmaker for the Decathlon set.

"Here we go," the nurse says, folding the footrests back down and lifting my feet onto them. I feel like a big baby once again, just like I did the day I walked into the free clinic near the school, worried about a bump on my head. "Wave good-bye to your friends."

I'm about to do just that when a familiar *whoosh* makes us all look at the double glass entrance doors to the ER as they slide open and Jane comes rushing in.

A little chill of recognition goes down my spine, because part of me feels like I'm reliving the night Derek died. But there's no fear on Jane's face this time, and no crazy scarf around her neck that she has to unwind like it's some kind of boa constrictor trying to strangle her. Also, I couldn't run away now like I did that night even if I tried. Before her eyes have a chance to find me, she calls out, "I'm Jane Greenwood, and I'm here for my friend. Where is she? Where's Brianna Taylor?"

19
always

I LIE ON a bed in room 22, holding the side railings for dear life as the nurse examines me down there with what feels like a monster claw instead of a hand. It's too late for them to give me an epidural, because I'm just *that much* too far dilated, she says, holding her thumb and index finger about half an inch apart. They give me a shot of something else instead, "just to take the edge off."

And there is no room for thought during the three hours that follow. There is only room for survival as I ride what feels like an ocean of pain and terror, with black waves the size of mountains that rise up out of the blue and then disappear, only to crash over my head again when I least expect it.

At one point I'm so worn out from the feeling of being split open that I simply lie back and try to die. The nurse holding one of my legs won't let me give up, though; she looks me right in the eye and says, "Now is the time to push. So get to it." And I want to cry because she's being so mean, but I don't even have the energy to do that.

So instead, I go ahead and just try to do what she says. I try to push, and pretty soon I figure out that as long as I'm willing to try, my body will do the rest.

And it's a perfect baby girl that comes out of me, everyone's dream of what a baby girl should be. I am still flat on my back when the nurse cuts the umbilical cord and brings the Bun close, and I don't even have the strength to lift my own head. I can see there is no end to the perfection of her, though, and my eyes take in every detail—from her squinched-up little eyes to her tiny fingers.

But then everything in the room seems to speed up—the machines, the people, even time itself—and I realize something's wrong. The doctor is giving orders, and all of a sudden there are more people there, moving things around and talking in code. What's mostly wrong is that the room is so quiet, even with all the talking and the voice coming over the hospital PA system requesting more assistance in room 22. It's quiet because the baby isn't making a sound.

"Why isn't she crying?" I ask no one in particular, since none of them are paying attention to me anyway at this point. Then: "Is she supposed to be that blue?"

"This happens sometimes with preemies," the nurse says as the doctor fits a tiny plastic oxygen mask over the Bun's face. "We're going to need to wrap the baby up and take her to the NICU."

"Where's that?" I say. "I want to go, too."

And all of a sudden it seems like everyone is moving a little *too* fast, like they're all in a little bit of a panic.

"It's the neonatal intensive care unit," the nurse says, keeping one eye on the doctor, who looks impatient as he takes the baby from her. "That sounds really scary, I know. But they have a warm little bed there with a tent that comes down so the baby can get all the oxygen she needs."

"We're going," the doctor says to her. "Now."

The nurse looks back at me as they're about to leave the room with my daughter. "It's all going to be okay," she says.

My mind flashes back to what Craig and Rose told me the day I first met them, how their little boy was born and then died before he even got a chance to live for a whole day. Is this what their nurse told them, too, that it was all going to be okay?

The nurse can see that I'm starting to pick up on the panic in the room, because her voice gets as firm as a librarian's as she starts to follow the doctor out the door but then turns around one last time. "Look me in the eye, Brianna. It's all going to be okay. Do you believe me?"

I nod, but I feel like I'm going to lose it. I'm exhausted and scared and mad that they're taking my baby away from me. *What gives you the right?* I want to scream at her. But I'm so tired that all I can say is "Bring her back to me when you're done. Please bring her back."

They don't bring her back for a long time, but the nurse was right: the baby is okay, and I'm moved to another room, where I'm supposed to recover from the birth. Like *that* is ever going to happen. I'm sorry, but pushing a human being out through your cupcake changes everything.

Jane has been out in the waiting room with Nate and Marjorie, and when she comes into the recovery room there are tears in her eyes.

"She's perfect, Brianna," she says, handing me a gift bag. Inside, wrapped in tissue, is a small stuffed dog that's had almost all its fur rubbed away.

"I came across it when I was going through a keepsake box. It was my favorite when I was little."

"I can tell," I laugh. Then, quietly, "Thank you, Jane. It means a lot."

Just then Marjorie and Nate come into the room. They're holding hands, and Nate hands me a little potted plant from the hospital gift shop. "We saw her through the glass," he says, smiling shyly—smiling the way high school guys tend to do when they're talking to . . . somebody's mom.

"They checked the Bun's heart when they were checking everything else," I tell them. "They tell me it's strong and beautiful."

Later, after everyone is gone and the Bun is back in room 22 with me, a nurse comes in every hour to check on us, until I finally just accept the fact that I am going to be a science experiment for the foreseeable future.

And then, around ten o'clock that night, when the Bun is finally asleep in her bassinet, Keisha calls my hospital room. "So Jolene and I are just hanging out here at my place," she says, "and I was thinking. If you and the baby need a place to stay or anything . . ."

At first I don't respond. I remember when I first showed up on Keisha's doorstep with nothing but my backpack and my long face. Then I remember the night when I stood on her front lawn with all my clothes strewn around me. Somewhere between those two moments, things changed between us.

I know I'll never forget what a good sister Keisha was to me when I was a little kid, and she was a good sister for taking me in when I wasn't so little. It's hard not to want to go running back to the fantasy of still having a sister like that. But Keisha can also be unpredictable and sketchy like our mother, and, like Jolene, she'll blow your world apart with a single good-bye if you let her.

And right at that moment I realize for the first time in my life that I've always thought Jolene and Keisha acted that way toward me because, somehow, I wasn't good enough, wasn't lovable enough. Now I realize it has nothing to do with me not being lovable, that maybe both their hearts were broken a long time ago and didn't heal quite right. That maybe they just don't know how to love very well themselves.

Finally, I just say, "Thanks, Keisha, but I think we're going to be okay."

It's my sister's turn not to respond, and after a few seconds of silence I hear Jolene in the background yelling out, "Tell her thanks a helluva lot for making me a grandma at my age."

After hanging up, I sit there and think for a few minutes. For the first time since I got to the hospital, there's total quiet in the room. No nurses coming in and out, no beeping machines, no voices over the speaker system. Just the sound of my own heart beating and the Bun making little suckling noises in her sleep. I push a little button on the remote control that raises the back of my hospital bed. Then I roll the Bun's bassinet close and gently lift her out so I can set her against my legs and just stare. Everything about her is so incredibly tiny—her fingers, her ears, and her mouth, which opens in this Gigantor yawn that makes me smile for the first time in what feels like forever.

And all of a sudden I'm thinking again about that month in foster care when Keisha and I were kids, how the CPS lady came to the house and Jolene screamed at her. "You have no right to take my babies away," Jolene cried, and I remember how bizarre it was, because she'd never acted like she really cared before then. She'd acted more like we were her property and she had a right to us. Sort of like how, lately, I've felt like I have a right to the Bun, who is looking me in the eye as if she's reading my thoughts.

I'm a mother now, I think. *I'll be a mother until the day I die.*

And then I whisper to the Bun. I whisper that life isn't about what I want anymore, because I want her more than I've ever wanted anything. Instead, it's about need—and not my need, but hers. She is perfect—a perfect, new little life—and no matter how badly I want to keep her all to myself, I know deep down that it wouldn't be the best thing for her.

"I will always love you more than I thought I could love anybody," I whisper to my little girl as the tears start to slip silently out of my eyes and down my cheeks, wetting her little pink blanket. "Always."

Then I pick up the phone next to my bed and dial Jane's number.

"Bree," she says, her voice clogged with sleep. "It's late. Are you okay? Is the baby okay?"

"We're fine," I tell her. "But I need you to do something."

"Anything."

I take a deep breath, and then I say, "I need you to call Craig and Rose."

20

epilogue: that particular miracle

I'M STANDING in front of the iron gate, getting ready to press the red PUSH FOR ENTRY button on the speaker box so Mo will buzz me through.

It's the end of my first month working at Hope House, and I remember so clearly that first day when I showed up at the gate after the Bun was born.

Mo answered, as usual.

"I saw your ad in the newspaper," I said as I stood in front of her desk. "The one for the child care position?"

At first, Mo just looked at me. No doubt she was still mad at me for lying to her about my real name and my age, and I was a little nervous to be standing there asking for a job. But then I thought back to last year, when I stayed at Hope House for a week. I thought of Angie and her kids—how Angie said she felt like she was a thousand years old sometimes. As Jane would say, I knew there was a need here, and I knew I could fill it. And that's exactly what I told Mo.

"You'll have to get your CPR certs," she finally said.

"I know."

"You also have to get fingerprinted down at the sheriff's office, since you'll be working with kids." She still wasn't being all warm and fuzzy, but at least she was talking to me.

"Thanks, Mo." I was trying to keep from grinning, because it didn't seem like the right time to let how happy I felt show on my face. So instead, I used the same words I'd said to Jane when she brought the worn-out plush dog from her childhood to the hospital: "It means a lot."

A week ago, I showed Mo my tattoo just before starting my shift, because she had relaxed a lot by then, and I could tell she was starting to trust me again.

"That's for my daughter," I said, pulling the neckline of my shirt down a little to show her the tiny star I'd had inked in just above my heart.

Even though they don't have to, Craig and Rose have been sending me pictures of Zoe, which is what they named my little girl—*their* little girl.

It means "Life," Rose wrote on the back of one of the pictures. *And she is the joy of our lives. You will never know, Brianna, just what kind of miracle you have been a part of.*

I still cry sometimes late at night from missing Zoe, but there are two things I've noticed about those times when my head and heart are filled with longing. The first is that I never regret bringing her into the world. The second is that I never regret letting her go.

After Zoe was born and I was released from the hospital, I stood in my room at Jane's house and looked around. It was time to put things away, like Jane had done with Derek's clothes. I thought back to the night Jane showed up at Hope House and told me she wanted to take me home with her, how I'd been totally insulted by her suggestion that I might actually need someone to help me. It seems laughable now: there was no bigger mess than Brianna Taylor back then, and yet I was so sure I was going to put my life back together without any help from anyone.

During my recovery from childbirth, Jane told me I was welcome to stay at her house as long as I wanted or needed to. So I knew it was time for me to do more than talk about paying rent; it was time for me to start contributing more—like an official renter—even though she still insisted it wasn't necessary. I was pretty sure Hope House wouldn't pay as well as some other places in town, but it would pay enough, and it was also the kind of summer job that would look good on the college applications I planned to send out in just a few months.

Because just this morning, while Jane was standing at the kitchen table going through yesterday's mail, she looked up at me and held out an envelope. "It's from the College Board," she said. "Your AP scores."

Thanks to Nate and his tutoring—and maybe to myself, too—the scores were pretty good.

"Dang, Brianna," Nate said when I called and told him.

Now, after signing in for the day and setting my time sheet on Mo's desk, I head out to the play yard, where the kids have set up a bunch of tumbling mats. The yard is hidden behind the back side of Hope House, with tall hedges surrounding it on all sides for privacy and protection. There are nine kids here at the moment, and most of them were here last week when I started showing them some cheerleading moves. I've already told the two boys and the oldest girl that they have the most important job on the squad: "You're spotters, which means it's your job to make sure your teammates are safe, okay?"

Jeffrey, who is six, points to the others and says, "I'm president of the Teenage Mutant Ninja Turtles, and I'm going to protect all you cheerleaders!"

The smallest girl is named Kate. She's an only child, and she's been here with her mother for almost three weeks. At first, Kate didn't want to talk, and her mother said she'd been like that since they arrived at Hope House.

"My daughter has seen things no child should have to see," Kate's mother told me that first day. She had her arms crossed tight in front of her chest like she was protecting her insides, and she turned away from where the kids were playing so they wouldn't see her blinking hard to get rid of the tears.

But then I noticed Kate watching the rest of us as we worked on a routine for a while, and when I asked her if maybe she wanted to join in, she nodded.

"Do you guys want me to show you how to make a human pyramid?" I ask the kids after all the mats have been set up. And then I have to shush them, since I'm pretty sure their enthusiasm can be heard a couple of towns over.

We talk about how it's going to go, and I use a piece of chalk on the concrete walkway to diagram a simple and safe basket toss variation. I draw a bunch of stick figures on all fours with one stick figure standing at the top of the pyramid. I add a triangle for her cheerleading skirt and then throw in some fluffy pom-poms.

"That's good," Kate says, and when I look at the stick-figure cheerleader standing up there all by herself, a part of me can't help thinking, *That used to be me: Brianna on the brink.*

Once the older base girls are in place, I help Kate step onto their backs and find her balance. The base girls start giggling at the way Kate's bare feet tickle, and I have to remind them not to squirm too much and lose their focus, or everyone will come tumbling down.

Mo is standing in the doorway with a cup of coffee in her hand, watching. "Go for it, Kate!" she says, winking at me.

I can tell Kate's nervous, though, because she looks right into my eyes and then down at the ground below, like maybe an easier way to get through this will be found down there.

"Kate," I say, getting her to focus on my eyes again. "Are you ready?"

At first she doesn't say anything, and I think she's going to ask me to help her down off the pyramid.

But then she closes her eyes for just a second, and when she opens them there's something different about her face. Something fearless. I can tell her mother sees it, too, because she lets her crossed arms relax a little, and there's a smile in her voice when she whispers, "That's my girl." And right then I remember how it feels when the fear goes away and you realize it's all going to be okay.

"*Wheeeeeeeee!*" Kate says as she spreads her arms wide and jumps from the backs of the two bigger girls. For a split second it's almost like she's floating there in midair, right above the spot where her mother and Jeffrey—the Turtle president—and I wait to help her land on her feet. And I smile as I remember how that moment feels. It's a feeling like no other, because all of a sudden you have wings.

All of a sudden, you're flying.